T

H

Cock

THCock

Stoner Boys

edited by

Bud Kush

UNZIPPED

Published in 2018 by Unzipped, an imprint of
Lethe Press, Inc.
6 University Drive • Suite 206 / PMB #223
Amherst, MA 01002 USA
www.lethepressbooks.com • lethepress@aol.com
ISBN: 978-1-59021-475-6 / 1-59021-475-7

The stories in this volume are works of fiction. Names,
characters, places, and incidents are products of the authors'
imagination or are used fictiously. Any resemblance to
actual events or locales or persons, living or dead, is entirely
coincidental.

Set in Warnock, Optima, and Baskerville.
Interior design: Alex Jeffers.
Cover design: Inkspiral Design.

Note from the editor:

We do not advise using these pages as rolling papers. Otherwise, enjoy!

Contents

"It was the hippies, the lifers and the juicers, and we all squared off nightly to find out pleasures, sometimes in a deserted bunker, sometimes downtown. I, of course, hung out with the hippies, and together we smoked dope and talked about peace and love and admiration…"

—*Memoirs of Dennis Peron*

"I think pot should be legal. I don't smoke it, but I like the smell of it."

—Andy Warhol

Lit Up

L.A. Fields

*E*li hesitates before he knocks, wondering if a polite rap of the knuckles is really appropriate this late at night, and this out of breath and frazzled, but there's probably no need to pound on the door and wake Nicky up—Nicky always says he loves the start of a new day so much he stays up to see every sunrise before he passes out. Eli tries knocking first. His hand glows unnaturally white in the dark against Nicky's apartment door. His knock seems even quieter than Eli meant it to be, coming after the extreme noise he made running up the metal steps to get here. The stairs are still humming under his feet. It's already been a hell of a night, and that's why he's run this errand to his drug dealer: to get the means by which he might chill the fuck out.

Nicky is already smirking before he opens the door. His short, brown hair is all licked up on one side like maybe he was sleeping at some point recently, though he doesn't look tired now. He looks amused, and his half-smashed hair doesn't even work against him because he's that handsome, the jerk.

"You've been standing here for like five minutes," Nicky says. "What are you, high?" He pulls a joint from behind his ear and sticks it in between his lopsided grin. It looks like a factory-produced cigarette, that's how carefully Nicky rolls his joints, with filters and everything. Eli wouldn't be surprised if Nicky had a tiny implement for tamping the leaves down, for building each cigarette like he would load a miniature canon. Such a thing could easily be around here somewhere, among all the other tiny tools and paraphernalia that litter this dim place.

"Not high," Eli says. "That's why I'm here. I've got money."

"You always have money," Nicky says, walking inside to let Eli follow him. "You just usually have it in the daytime." Eli shuts the door and sits down in the chair with a couple of burns on the arms, the only one Nicky lets his dirtbag drug-buying friends sit and smoke in. That's the seat Eli takes, because that's what he's here to do.

Nicky lights the joint in his mouth, and then hands it to Eli with eyebrows that say, *Yeah?* There's a gleam on the highest arch—a brow piercing—and tattoos peppering his upper body, but with no balance or reason to their placement; one bicep, right wrist, left shoulder blade, a few ribs, several knuckles, and something on the back of his neck. The ones with words are either misspelled or badly phrased, but Eli knows not to point that out; being too smart seems like a quick way to not be sold any drugs.

"What do you want?" Nicky asks, heading back into the dark recesses of his apartment. Eli calls out his order and sticks the damp end of Nicky's joint in his mouth, gets two merciful puffs in before Nicky returns with a baggie. He opens it so Eli can see and smell its contents, seals it back up and weighs it in front of him, takes Eli's money from his hand before setting the bag in his palm, and Eli pockets it while Nicky counts the cash and tucks it somewhere in the many knickknacks on his coffee table. That chore accomplished, the only thing left to tidy up is the matter of this burning roach, which they'll certainly finish together. Nicky sits down on his couch and they start passing it back and forth, beneath the light of the end table's lamp, which stands lit between them.

"Rough night?" Nicky asks.

"Yes," Eli says, but doesn't elaborate. The pot is starting to take effect, and he becomes rather literal, reserved, and mute when he's high. Nicky does not.

"You're not usually one to keep odd hours, are you?" He's wearing socks and boxers and never more if he's at home, never jeans or a shirt, even when it's cold. He only gets dressed when he legally must if he wants to go outside without getting harassed or arrested for indecency. "Usually the people who come to me at night are coming down off of something else, impulsive, you know? But you're not one of them, you've always seemed like a college kid. Which you are, right? Or you were when you started coming around. Have you graduated yet?"

"Last year." Nicky's got to be about Eli's age, maybe a year or two older, but for sure he has never gone to college.

"And studied what? I'd study science if I were you. I don't know what kind you'd like, chemistry or biology or what, but for me: I'm good at math, and I like knowing how things work. I like making shit grow, too, but I don't like, like, *purposeless* math, fucking theoretical doesn't-add-up math, and science can get messy too, with all those chemicals. I'd rather keep it practical and organic. Math that makes sense like grams and money, you know? Plants, herbs, cash, anything that's green."

"I studied sociology."

"That's almost science, good for you. What's Eli short for, is that Elias or Elijah or were you named after Eli Manning and that's just your whole name?" Nicky talks with his hands a bit, and when he's holding the joint, the smoke of it starts to draw brief shapes in the air, like the ultimate temporary tattoo.

"Eliot."

"Like the dragon!" Nicky says with a full smile that he runs his tongue over. Everything is moving like a flashback on TV to Eli now. His powers of observation are uselessly focused on every slow detail, and so he knows: Nicky is thinking of Pete's Dragon, and of Puff the Magic Dragon at the same time, probably, but like those incorrect tattoos, Eli doesn't point out these observations either.

"The poet."

"Hmm, I don't know that one. You want to know what Nicky's short for? Most people assume Nicholas of course, and one Greek guy I knew had like seventeen Nicky names—Nicodemus, Nikandros, Nicotine, whatever. But my name ends with Nick, it doesn't start with Nick, can you guess it?"

"Is it just plain Nick, and that's your whole name?" Eli asks, repeating Nicky's question from before, though Nicky seems to have already forgotten what he's said: he talks so much he must just live in the moment, only knowing what he's saying as it comes spilling out of his mouth. His mouth has to stay in constant motion for him to breathe, to live. He's like a hummingbird maybe, or a shark.

"No, you idiot, but that's not the worst guess—one guy asked me if my name was Yannick. Who the fuck's name is Yannick? Not mine, that's for sure. I'm Dominick, and people when they know that, they always ask me why I didn't go with Dom, but I don't like the sound of it, do I? I mean it sounds too fucking gay, doesn't it? And I'm more of a sub anyway."

Eli says nothing, because that wasn't a question, so he doesn't have to answer for it. He takes the offered joint though, and notices that the filter on this one is made from a bit of card paper, with a folded bit in the tube that's shaped like W, which stands for Weed, one would assume.

"How are you with sex and getting high?" Nicky goes on, his posture strung and taught, sitting on the edge of his seat while

Eli feels slumped in his chair with hardly the strength to lift his smoking arm. "Me, I'm ready to go all the time, but I guess some guys get like the pot version of whiskey dick, their mind just isn't in the game at all even if they can get hard, and some can't get hard, they just shut off. You look like you're in a trance right now, do you shut off?"

"No," Eli says. "I buzz." Eli's dick does get hard when he's high, he can tell it's about to do so right now, since Nicky's glancing down at his crotch looking for a tent in his pants, and Eli's dick likes attention, the way his skin likes to lie out in the sun on the first day of summer. Eli's *mind* shuts off when he's high, drops down to sweet, simple, basic processing, but his skin feels hand-slapped and stung when it's a good high—it's like being made out of TV static, or like when his foot falls asleep: though it can still feel most things, it doesn't quite read them the same way.

Eli's body can still move as it usually does when he's toasted like this, but it becomes all the more interesting to touch because it's ever so slightly altered. He hands the joint back to Nicky and wonders vaguely why the static he feels doesn't cause a zap between their fingers during the hand-off.

"What do you call this color?" Nicky asks, reaching out to touch Eli's hair. He's flirting now, and has been since he started talking about Eli's dick's habit on drugs for sure. Now the hot skin of his fingers touches Eli's hair where it's long, at the top, and brushes over his forehead. "I mean I know it's red, I'm not fucking blind, but what kind do you call this shade? Girls always think that they're strawberry or copper, no matter what it actually looks like. There's fake red that looks like Kool-Aid, and then gingers and carrot tops, but I think those are ugly; cartoon-orange hairs are the ones who look splattered with freckles like it's dried blood, but you don't have any of that."

"I'm rusty," Eli says.

"Yeeeaaaaahh," Nicky says with a bro-y drawl, combing Eli's hair a bit now, rubbing it through his fingers like it's a fabric he's considering for a garment. "Yeah, that's your color, it's nice."

"Thank you."

Now Nicky takes a quick puff of the joint, which is about out, and presses it to Eli's lips with all four of his fingers, like he wants to blow someone a kiss but can't spare one, and needs to borrow a kiss off Eli. He takes his hand away after that, but stays leaned in close.

"So what's up with you tonight, why are you here so late?"

Eli inhales on the joint where it dangles from his lips, then takes it down to answer.

"I set something on fire, and I was getting jittery about it, and I thought I had some weed at home so I could calm down and put myself to bed, but I was out." Literal to a fault on pot, that's what Eli is; he answers every question he's asked without agenda, just to state the facts as he knows them.

"What'd you set on fire? Was it something you're allowed to set on fire, like fireworks or a candle? Or like were you burning some old taxes files in a trashcan and it got out of control before you put it out with a cup of tea or something? You would get paranoid and dramatic about something so innocent, you seem like that type. Or did you go *really* crazy for some reason, and now you're here because you *snapped*, and now you're like a super calm psycho? Did you burn down a building, somebody's house, or just start a forest fire by flinging a lit butt into the woods?"

"No," Eli says. He's just answering the last question he's heard; he couldn't keep up with the rest of it if he tried, and his thoughts are getting sluggish now that the joint is nearly down to the end. Eli hands it back to Nicky, lets him deal with putting it out, which he does, and stows it away in a mint tin on his end table, full of other butt-ends for later repurposing.

Nicky comes back to Eli after that's done, closer this time, and sets his head against Eli's shoulder. Eli wonders if he's listening for a heartbeat when Nicky inhales deeply.

"You don't smell like gasoline," Nicky says, "or even smoke, are you sure you're some pyro? Are you a hot-head, huh? Hair red like fire?"

Eli touches Nicky's head reflexively, he can't not cradle a head pressed to his chest; it begs to be held. He finds that touching Nicky's skin, his face, is like rubbing a balloon against long hair: there's a natural cling to this contact.

"Burnt orange," he says, close to Nicky's ear like he's telling him a secret. That's the kind of red hair joke Nicky wants to make now. "I got into a fight with my boyfriend and turned dinner over on the stove. Gas burners, open flame, grease fire maybe, but fuck him. I hope the curtains catch and his whole place goes up."

"What did he do?" Nicky asks. He started kissing Eli's neck the second he said "boyfriend," and Eli doesn't stop him. His dick feels as big and throbbing with blood as his neck right now, as if they're both the same, pulsing and thick.

"He wanted to see other people, and he thought he could do that and still keep me happy, like I was the asshole if I didn't want to add more fun to our relationship."

Nicky's hands have slid down Eli's back, peeling a space between him and the chair. Nicky's hands smooth over his ribs and land on his hip bones. He's nibbling at Eli's neck now, which is good; the occasional pinch of a bite wakes him out of a full pot-numbed stupor, keeps him present. Eli opens his mouth to let a lock of Nicky's stuck-up hair between his lips. He feels like a baby panda eating leaves, but it's a feeling he likes just fine.

"You don't want to see other people?" Nicky asks, lifting up his head to look into Eli's eyes, and then kiss him on the mouth. When the kiss starts, Eli closes his eyes. What he wanted earlier this evening is irrelevant now, that's not where he is anymore.

Now he's here and comfortable in Nicky's arms, and he won't turn down this embrace. "Are you sure?" Nicky asks after the kiss is finished. Eli drags his eyes back open, but at last he feels no need to answer this question. It's time to start asking his own questions.

"Do you want to open up my pants?" Eli asks, and Nicky answers him by doing it, with fingers so nimble they seem to blur. Time blips out for Eli—it's like what he says goes from request to fulfillment in an instant.

Nicky starts sucking his dick right away, manic and fast about everything, about talking and touching and twisting up those clever goddamn filters, and now this. There are a bunch of pre-made filters ready to go in a basket on his coffee table, like pot-pourri or potato chips; Nicky must make those things like other people make origami or twist their hair or knit, a way to keep his hands busy while watching television or whatever.

Eli takes one of Nicky's hands and tucks it under his shirt, so Nicky can twiddle one of his nipples like it's a radio dial. He sets his other hand on the top of Nicky's head, encouraging his mouth to sink lower. Eli closes his eyes and feels like the chair is starting to pleasantly consume him again. The hand in Nicky's hair feels indifferently numb now, which is all the better for the sake of concentrating on what Nicky's doing with his mouth.

He wasn't kidding about being a sub, he seems to be enjoying himself on the same level Eli might if he was performing some kind of controlled acrobatic feat, something that involved muscling deliberately around a phallic shape: flexing a routine over a pommel horse, or stroking circles around the yank and tug of the uneven bars, flying between them and catching his own momentum each time.

With one hand still tweaking Eli's nipple, the other makes its way up Eli's chest, claps around his neck for a moment, and then starts to play with his earlobe. Eli feels like he's being held by the thinnest strings, a puppet to Nicky's controlling tugs. Eli summons up enough strength to buck his hips away from the pull of the chair, and this pleases Nicky, or at least makes him moan and drop his fingerwork to grab Eli's ass and yank him closer so he can sit back on his heels comfortably while he sucks him off.

"Whoa, Nicky," Eli says, wanting to warn him that he's close enough to the edge already, prepared to climax at any moment into the slick warmth of Nicky's gullet, and maybe he doesn't want to do that yet? But Nicky just puts a hand over Eli's mouth again to shut him up, and Eli starts to lip around until he can get Nicky's ring and middle finger into his mouth, to suck him in return. When he reaches the moment of completion, he bites down as gently as he can on Nicky's fingers, riding out the orgasmic twist of ejaculation. He also vaguely imagines that, were he to bite down too hard, Nicky's fingers would feel wonderful sliding down the back of his throat, swallowed whole.

But the fingers slip out through his mouth still attached to their owner, and Eli lazily opens his eyes to see Nicky tucking his pants back into place.

"Now what?" he asks Nicky.

"Tell me you want to stay the night," Nicky says.

Eli nods. He gets invited back to the inner sanctum of Nicky's place, where before now he wouldn't have been allowed to even use the bathroom. He undresses and folds his clothes by dropping them down slowly onto an unmarked cardboard box in Nicky's room so they'll accordion into a neat stack. The walls of this room are lined with boxes and shelves full of more boxes, along every wall including behind the bed. Eli gets into this bed with his underpants on even though Nicky strips down to nothing before crawling in first. Eli doesn't ever sleep in the nude, and he doesn't know this guy that well, does he, regardless of recent events? When Eli joins him, Nicky leans over him to turn off the bedside lamp, and then stays on top of him, skin-to-skin, to fall sleep.

Eli enjoys this. He doesn't want to start thinking too much again until he absolutely must, and that moment is not tonight, when he can let his mind fuzz over and drift away, knowing nothing but the weight of Nicky's oddly inked body.

In the murky night, when his mind is still half-foggy, Eli wakes to Nicky kissing his neck. He stirs enough to make out with him, thinking this will lead to something more, and so is surprised when Nicky stops abruptly just as they get going. Nicky lies back on his side of the bed, under the window's glow of street- and moonlight, and only looks at Eli, watches him with eyes so expectant that Eli feels compelled to do something about it.

Turning onto his elbows, Eli army-crawls until he's overtop of Nicky, and he looks down at him as shrewdly as he can, to make sure this is what the guy wants. He pins one arm across Nicky's chest, and with the other reaches down to bring up one of Nicky's knees, to open up his legs. Nicky's face softens, and Eli feels his own expression harden—gentle curiosity being replaced with a stern task.

"You want it like this?" Eli asks.

Nicky's only response is to reach behind him onto the closed surfaces of those boxes he uses like an extended countertop, and he tosses a wrapped condom at Eli's chest, where it bounces to land back on Nicky. Eli goes to work unwrapping and applying the thing, while Nicky goes rummaging for a bottle of lube with a pump top. When Eli's done, Nicky nods to indicate the bottle, and pumps a squirt of the stuff into Eli's hand when he proffers it.

Everything he does to Nicky is embraced and drawn closer. He starts to fuck him, and Nicky hooks his ankles together behind Eli's back to make him do it harder. Kissing turns to biting, and biting cedes to hair-pulling, then hair-pulling to clawing, and by the next morning when they wake up sticky with one another, there are marks of their night on both their bodies, between Nicky's tattoos and over Eli's freckles. Eli notices them when he wakes up, before averting his eyes and trying to stare a hole through the ceiling.

Because it's the next day! So the reel that went out the night before comes spooling back into Eli's clear head. He knows bitterly that he'll have marks noticeable above his clothes when he goes to work on Monday, he can *feel* places of raw tenderness all over him. Hickies for sure, maybe even scratch marks with the perfect spacing that lets everyone know a human caused them and not a fall or a pet. What the hell *was* last night? He can't just break up with someone, he's got to cause a scene of destruction, too? Can't go home after that and cry himself to sleep or something, he has to get high? And even that can't put him to bed, it puts him in his dealer's bed, *really*? This grease ball with his room full of boxes like he just moved in when he's been here for years, what's in them? Probably nothing good.

"Don't start thinking of opening any of my boxes," Nicky says, when he gets up to go to the bathroom. He comes back after the sound of a flushing toilet, wiping his hands on his shorts. "You want breakfast? What do you like for breakfast, salt or sugar? Tell me, I'll get you some breakfast."

Getting breakfast from Nicky doesn't mean going out, nor does it mean Nicky goes out to get it alone so that Eli can sneak out, nor does he cook. Nicky calls someone he knows is headed over for a regularly scheduled drug buy, and says the guy can have an extra joint out of Nicky's own stash if he picks up their order of food. The guy agrees, and Eli doesn't want to meet whoever does such errands for his dealer, nor does he imagine that guy wants to meet the piece of trash who fucks said dealer, so Eli stays in Nicky's bed, dressed the way Nicky usually is in his shorts only, waiting.

The voice of the person who brings breakfast is female, and Nicky comes back in with some breakfast burritos and milk-shakes saying, "She wanted to know if you were cute, did you hear what I told her?"

"No," Eli says. He doesn't care. He wonders if Andy, that's his boyfriend, or was his boyfriend up until last night most likely, has done anything over the past few hours. Did he have to call the fire department because Eli flipped his dinner over onto the stove? Did he use his spare key to break into Eli's place and steal shit or wreck shit or even just take back his stuff and leave a nasty note where Eli's roommate will find it first?

"I said you were red-hot, and that the carpet matched the drapes," Nicky says.

Eli puts his head in his hand, trying to cover his eyes from it all.

"Oh, come on, it's not that bad a joke, don't be an asshole," Nicky says, joining Eli cross-legged on the sheets.

"It's not that, I mean…that is the most obnoxious joke to all redheads, but I just…I hate my life right now, but I bet I'll hate it more if I really did set my boyfriend's apartment on fire."

"Ex-boyfriend, isn't he?" Nicky asks with his half a grin. He's chewing his food with the other half of his mouth.

Eli shrugs, wondering if he should start worrying that Nicky's some psychotic possessive type—he *is* a drug dealer, after all; Nicky could easily be unstable and violent. But then…Eli's the one flipping fire around people's houses, so who the hell knows. Eli tries to take a bite of his food and thinks the cheesy egg mix is about the consistency of a sick person's clotted snot, and then he doesn't want to eat anymore. Nicky hands him his milkshake and that goes down easier, cold and sugary, and after a few sips of that he feels ready to attempt eating again.

"Chill the fuck out," Nicky says, touching Eli's shoulder with a hand that's cold and wet from the condensation on his drink.

It's still pretty nice to have Nicky's hands on him. Whatever else went wrong last night, the sex was good. He puts his hand over Nicky's and slides it further up his arm, appreciating the muscle under his skin, the way he would appreciate lifting up a section of a python, nothing but dense, smooth power. "Finish your food and we'll take a walk, okay? If the place burnt down we'll be able to tell, and if it didn't, then you can stop worrying, all right?"

Eli rolls his eyes. As if his worrying can be stopped by logic and facts, there's always more to worry about! He can stop worrying when he sees the building and checks his own apartment and calls a locksmith to change the locks and makes sure his roommate gets the new key and then gets some response from Andy that assures him there are no hard feelings—Andy's the one who wanted to see other people, right? So as long as he feels like *he's* the one who broke up, and never finds out about Nicky, then maybe Eli can stop worrying, if he has some drugs on hand to help the cause.

The walk with Nicky makes Eli feel as conspicuous as a criminal, because in a couple of senses he is one, and he's certainly associating with one. Eli retraces the route he took the night before, this time with Nicky at his side quieter than ever, too busy observing his surroundings to talk, maybe some pot-induced paranoia on his part, or maybe he has reason to be paranoid, it could go either way. Eli spots Andy's building and is pleased to see it isn't a charred ruin. Nothing is wrong with it, and the one person who happens to be leaving it doesn't look as if they spent the night on the sidewalk waiting for the fire department to clear the area. It looks like nothing happened. Probably nothing happened.

"There you go, huh?" Nicky says when Eli looks to him, sheepish in knowing he's done all this emotional flailing for nothing. "Practically songbirds and shit around here, you didn't do anything but make a mess."

Nicky nudges Eli with his elbow, both hands stuck in his pockets until they start walking again. Then he puts an arm around Eli's shoulders.

"What's up?" Eli asks, wondering why Nicky's so chummy. Shouldn't he have kicked Eli out the morning after a hook-up and told him to get lost? What's all this breakfast buddy stuff?

"Why don't you come by my place tomorrow?"

"What for?"

"The pleasure of my company, stupid. I'm asking you out but I hate going out, you know? And you and what's-his-name are done, right? You haven't said yes or no yet."

"I guess so," Eli says. Weird. That was sudden, but it's true.

"So how about me? You want a dreamboat drug dealer? A prince of the projects?"

"Royalty, are you?"

"Gutter royalty," Nicky says, a full smile stretching across his face. He's kidding, but he does hold his head up with pride when he speaks of himself like this, with his trash titles.

"All right," Eli agrees in the same way he sometimes (rarely) says, *Fuck it.* "What time?"

"Not early," is as specific as Nicky wants to be about their plans.

"Okay, well then, I promise I won't be late," Eli says. He's about to smirk himself, he can feel it coming on. What, are smirks communicable now? Like herpes, or mono? Nicky snorts.

"Okay, funny guy, go break up with that loser. See you tomorrow."

After a moment of pleasant disbelief and watching him saunter away, Eli does what Nicky says. He goes up to Andy's apartment and stands before his door. This morning, at this door, in this moment, his knock does not hesitate.

His First Time

Alex Jeffers

[Excerpted from a work in progress]

"I was ten," Ggau said, "when I swore never to cut my hair. Very fierce and ferocious and righteous. And ignorant and stupid."

It was dark, with a less than quarter moon off to the west toward the Pelles. In the lee of the massy Sudhin peninsula, halfway from that city at its tip to the main bulk of Eü, the sheltered sea lay flat and quiet, fragrant with salt and kelp, benignly rocking anchored *Foambreaker*. From here were no great destinations before Yn: fishing ports of the Treft peoples, then the outlying Pellestri isles. *Foambreaker* would stop in where trade flags were raised or bonfires burning, though pickings were notoriously slim in Treft. Six or seven more days.

"Grandda was...imprecise about what happened to him, what impelled him to flee Daewen. What I understood was that he was a prince—his grandson, *I*, was a prince. Fide, lovely, you won't understand what that meant."

"I suppose not," dryly murmured the son of the late monarch of Vorsest.

"In all the world I knew were only two people with black skin: Mother and me. They weren't cruel, the children I knew in town and on the vineyard—not like the brats at the conservatory later. But I couldn't ever forget, wasn't permitted to forget, how different I was. I was the outlandish black boy whose mother and father wouldn't live in the same house together—wouldn't live within twenty thousand paces of each other. And too wealthy for some, with Da's vineyard on one side and Mother's businesses on the other. Much better, much much more satisfactory, to be exiled prince of a distant mountain realm, dispossessed by a wicked sorcerer."

Deploying in nearly equal measures charm and bluster, Ggau had secured the nook in *Foambreaker*'s prow for them for the night. He wanted air and breeze and stars about. Sailors being a romantic lot, he'd been prepared to mutter vague words about a marriage in the offing, though it was surely unlucky so early, but it hadn't come to that. They were gravely promised perfect privacy.

Ggau'd dragged up mattress and pillows from the aft port cabin. A plate of sliced salt sausage and Sudhin cheeses, olives, lemons. Two bottles of his da's green wine provided from her private stash by quizzical Meffer, and three made-up batons of dreamleaf. "He's not to—auw! a shallow sniff or three wun't harm him if he wants it. Listen to his cough. You'll know if it goes bad." A supply of candles for the two glass chimneys.

"Grandda didn't say.... I think I'm only realizing now he never said what vow he made when he walked away from Skhekhrio, only that he said it and never after cut his hair. He can't have been much older than I was, a child himself, maybe sixteen. And he didn't say—the sorcerer did something awful to him. So awful he wouldn't speak. But the worst was, he and the awful thing together were just a tool for the sorcerer to control Grandda's big brother as he already controlled their mother who ruled the clans of Daewen. And it didn't *matter* Grandda walked away, the sorcerer had his tool. Grandda couldn't ever save his brother, it was too late. I think, Fide, I think he loved his brother the way you loved Sech."

Fide's warm arm against Ggau's had gone tense. He said nothing for a long moment, then, "It's time to drink. I feel I dislike this sorcerer a very great deal. At least my fucking big brother had compassion sufficient to *kill* Sech."

"Are you well, precious Fide?"

"Handsome Ggau, I've been ill a stinking tedious long while but under Meffer's watchful eye and in your tender care I'm getting better. I won't get blind drunk—"

"Because I won't permit it."

"Because my ferocious Ggau won't permit it. But I'd like a cup of your da's green. My mouth tastes foul. Royals and sorcerers!"

Ggau reached for a bottle. "Do you know, we don't have them in the Pelles. Royals. Sorcerers either, that I know, but I expect if they didn't want me to I wouldn't."

A hand touched his brow, traced a fingertip the length of his nose. "Ggau. Don't do this. Don't get distracted and irrelevant. I know—I believe I know how difficult it is. You may get blind drunk if it'll help."

Setting the bottle down unopened, Ggau drew lingering fingers to his mouth. "It wouldn't," he whispered into Fide's hand, "but I may." He laced their fingers together, squeezed. "Most of this I've never said to anybody. A lot of it I never actually *thought*, just did. So I don't know if it'll make sense. But you're right to make me say it. You— Fide!" A horror had spiked up in his throat with the sour jaggedness of vomit. "I meant to make you my tool as the sorcerer did my grandda!"

Ggau experienced the barest pause before Fide spoke, while Fide thought, as centuries.

"You didn't, though. You haven't yet. I believe you've been fighting against committing that...violation with all your considerable might right from the start, without even knowing it."

"Do you see—" Giddy with relief, with benediction, Ggau dragged Fide up into his embrace. "*This* is why I must say it. To you! Because I only ever *do* things, like a ten year old. You're not like that."

"It's true," said Fide wickedly, "you mashed your ass up against my cock while I might still be dilly-dallying now."

Ggau pecked Fide's cheek, temple, brow, released him. "Now *you're* off the subject."

"The subject was wine."

"You're clever, and aggravating, and perfectly lovely," said Ggau, reaching again for the bottle.

"You're aggravating, and so beautiful I can't abide it, and don't get me started on what I adore in you, Kholtenggau Zigaro, because I will never stop and it will be unbearably tedious."

"Really?" Ggau's mind had gone absolutely flat with astonishment.

"Beauty first, because I have eyes." Flopping back into the pillows, Fide sighed. "But yes, really, I admire several other of your aspects and talents in addition. We'll commence with your generosity of spirit, and there we'll stop because I'll turn to porridge and sound like an especially jejune love story of the sort I read too many of as a youth."

Not trusting himself, Ggau poured one cup nearly full, then the other. He handed the first across Fide's supine chest for him to take and mumbled, "I'm thinking. I might be thinking a while but I promise we'll get back to cases. You may toss knives at me if I don't." He sipped from his own cup. "I'll sniff some 'leaf as well. Help me make connections, do you see. Would you undo my hair?"

"Ggau?"

"I just—I feel I want it loose for a while. And I want you to loose it."

"I will, then. I'm honored by the request."

"Hush. It's not an honor, it's a chore."

Ggau reached up a baton from the tray. By the time he had it lit deliberate fingers were exploring the club of braided hair on his nape, working out its structure and connections. His thoughts were…strangely unlike thoughts. Not words, images, perceptions—or words, images, and perceptions compressed so small and tossed about so rapidly they couldn't be tracked. His mind clickety-clicked like his mother's fingers on her abacus. Fide found the one link, fiddled it loose. Club unreeled into plait down Ggau's spine, thumping as it went. Redistribution of its weight provoked interesting sensations. "I should have brought up my comb," Ggau said. "I'm sorry."

"I have fingers."

Ggau felt each glance of those fingers at the base of his spine, teasing the braid apart from the bottom, like a loving blow. On his nape the root shifted minimally but perceptibly left-right, left-right. Clickety-click. Sniff. He hadn't coughed yet. "Meffer said you may try the 'leaf if you like."

"Hmm-hah." The fingers hardly slowed to think. "When I finish this, then, I'd like."

"I didn't tell Grandda I'd made a vow, though it was on his behalf. I suppose because he'd think I thought he failed his own. Now I consider, Fide, you're maybe the third person I ever told. *By mountain iron that binds the Land Below the Land, by lightning in the clouds that binds the Sky Above the Sky, by glacier ice that binds the Sea Beneath the Sea, I will not cut my hair before I've slain the sorcerer who plagues my grandda's country.* I didn't know at ten, do you see, the name of that country or what the sorcerer calls himself. Grandda never said. I didn't have a notion in creation what a glacier was. I knew the proper word for oaths, though, not *kill* but *slay*. I'd had some practice with blades, people who knew a bit said I had talent. I felt certain, because I was ten, talent, more training, and a great whacking sword were all I'd need, because it was a virtuous, glorious, heroic deed I meant to do.

"I took what instruction I could find in Yn. It's a perishingly peaceful place for the most part so that was mostly foreigners and sailors happy to take coin from an eager boy. Useless, much of it. Da gave me his old cutlass from when he sailed with Meffer, as a joke really, I think, and to annoy Mother. When I—

"My first kill, Fide. I was twelve. Mother and I were on the docks. She still hoped to interest me in trade. I say I take after her but it's just the coloring, she's a tiny thing, I was already taller. She came out of a shop. I was a little slower because there was a fascinating case of knives. A big, stupid brute off some ship had an arm up under her chin so her feet dangled off the ground and broke her wrist getting her to drop her little stiletto. *Little black monkey whore,* he kept calling her. So I hamstrung him with Da's cutlass before he knew I was there. He really was stupid. It was so easy I didn't need to know anything, blade work, anatomy, nothing. After he collapsed and Mother scuttled away I blunted the cutlass trying to chop his head off. Blind rage and terror. *Hundreds* of witnesses. I was a hero. Nobody *likes* Mother but everybody respects her."

"Ggau." Fide's fingers had paused halfway up his spine. "How did you feel?"

"After? Well, I threw up. I think everybody does. And then for days, nothing. Nothing at all. As if I'd killed the part that feels along with that stupid foreign sailor." Ggau took a sniff of Meffer's suave 'leaf. "Then Mother sat me down for what she called a conference. Her arm in a sling, wrist splinted and wrapped, spine stiff like a sword with not enough play in it, and this air of…disappointment." Clickety-click. "You'll find Qaziyeh's always disappointed about *something*. I wasn't to think she was ungrateful, she started. It was a pity I'd killed the man, was all. Somebody somewhere must have valued him. Crippling him was more than sufficient. Then that I was to go out to the vineyard for a while.

"It's most of a day's walk. I had plenty of time to think. Understand, I can't trust myself around my mother. I hear things she doesn't say. What I heard was: *Clumsy little black monkey boy can't get it right, can't be trusted in town.* By the time I got to Da's house I was feeling again and it was all resentment. Damn that man for being so easy to kill. Damn Mother for attracting his attention. Damn Da's cutlass for being a lousy blade—if I'd killed him *neatly* maybe it wouldn't be such a fault. Damn me for not knowing what I was *expected* to do when somebody attacked her.

"Then, at Da's, I was a hero all over again but also a—well, a thug. Ulm particularly—he's Da's live-in fellow. I felt he was nervous of me. *Big black monkey boy, chop me up as soon as look at me.* I confess I never took to Ulm. Da has dismayingly poor taste in who he tumbles into his bed, to my mind."

"Your grandfather?"

"Dead. I didn't say? Half a year before. Half-crippled with the bone fever for years, never quite happy since his wife died, a drunk. Heart gave out."

Pushing the last little length of intact plait aside (loosed hair tickled Ggau's back through shirt and jerkin), Fide laid his cheek to Ggau's spine and gripped his shoulders. "Nobody to tell you you'd wounded yourself killing the man, no guidance as to how to heal."

"I'm well over it now but I feel in some ways I regret that kill more than any of the later ones. Are you ready for your first sniff of 'leaf?"

"Just a few more tugs," Fide said, returning to work. "I haven't hurt you? Your hair is wondrous, Kholtenggau."

"There's a lot of it." Seeing the baton had gone out, Ggau set it down for now and retrieved his wine cup.

"Wondrous. Soft and strong and richly colored."

"What? It's black."

"So is a raven's plumage until you look. I'm sorry, Ggau, but the fact is you are beautiful and your hair sublime."

Clickety-click. "You *will* say that. Am I to believe it? Striking, I've been called. Impressive. Exotic—fucking *exotic*. Loud. Largely bearded. Savagely hirsute. A big prick and some skill with it. A big *sword* and some skill." Ggau coughed as if from a sniff of rough dreamleaf. "Big. Black. Monkey. Boy."

"Bar the last," said Fide calmly, "all of those are certainly true of my Ggau. As first impressions they'll serve. My impressions are no longer *first*. To me you are simply and complexly beautiful, of face, of form, of mind, of spirit."

Urgently reaching over his own shoulder, Ggau clasped, stilled one of Fide's hands. "Do you know? This is not a new thought. My Fide has a—a *magical* habit of bringing to light my deepest-buried anxieties which I've walled away behind bluster and joviality, and soothing me of them. I…will be beautiful if you command it."

"If it's a command you require, you have it." With two brisk tugs Fide broke Ggau's plait fully apart, ran clawed fingers through to the ends. "I'll take more wine but save the 'leaf for a bit. And I'll sit where I may see your face, Kholtenggau, for I intend to speak intimately."

"I shall turn," said Ggau. "Am I alarmed?"

"I imagine you ought to be."

Cross-legged on the mattress, they faced each other, wine cups in hand. With his free hand, Fide brushed a wisp of gleaming black head hair out of Ggau's beard, back over his shoulder. Running fingertips down Ggau's arm, he grasped that hand, lifted it to his lips. "This *magic* of mine. You have it in equal measure.

I'm perhaps less demonstrative when you dig my fears up to reveal I'm capable of facing them—"

"You're a less noisy fellow than I all around," said smiling Ggau.

"It's insight, not magic. It's caring. It's recognizing each other: how we're similar and different and how our differences are complementary. We're damaged people, Ggau. I suppose everybody is but you and I have been particularly damaged. It's a never-ending wonder we can function at all."

Clickety-click. "You managed for years because you had one overmastering goal."

"I would not fucking *permit* my fucking brother to kill me. Yes, I think so."

"How will you manage now you're free and safe?"

"It will be years, I expect, before I fully believe I am."

"You think my...my organizing principle is that ten year old's melodramatic vow."

"You haven't convinced me it isn't."

"Auw! You're inconvenient! You're aggravating! I will kiss you!"

Two wine cups went flying. Somehow neither broke. Ggau discovered he was not so fearful of breaking Fide and that Fide had rediscovered how to fight back. "My lovely Fide," Ggau panted after a good long breathless while, "I do believe you're nearly well."

"I'm all bruises!"

Ggau hurriedly sat up. "No."

"Exceedingly happy and contented and well earned bruises. I'm perhaps *almost* nearly well. I feel, if you asked me to walk from your mother's to your father's house, I would perish, but a quarter the distance handily survive. Without falling down. Unless, of course, some unconscionably beautiful rogue pops out of the undergrowth to knock me over."

Ggau placed his palm on Fide's heaving belly. "Only so as to pick you up again."

"I know."

"Will I lift you upright?"

Fide lazily smirked. "If you would."

Pillows were arranged, Fide propped up among them, a kiss offered and received. "Will I pour wine?"

"Please."

"At this time," said Ggau, contemplative, rousting cups from their skulking places, "my dearest wish is for you to be well. It's a misery knowing you miserable. Yet I find—" a filled cup was pushed into Fide's hand—"I find I take great comfort from caring for you. It's a paradox."

"I find my dearest wish, dearest Ggau, is that there should be no need for you to care for me yet you'd continue doing so."

"Goes without saying."

"And permit me, you superbly competent man, to care for you."

"As you do." With quiet joy Ggau smiled. "As you already do."

Feeling scarcely any trepidation, Ggau retrieved the half-consumed baton of dreamleaf and a witch's candle to relight it. He straddled Fide's hips on his knees, not requiring him to take any weight. "You'll observe the method," he said around the baton between his teeth, pinching candle alight, "and exercise excessive caution when your turn comes. You wish to draw the smoke into your lungs but, the first sniff, I think, only into your mouth." With the baton pinched between thumb and forefinger, he opened wide to show smoke coiling upon his tongue. He breathed it out. "I guarantee you won't like it, to start, it's an unnatural act and the flavor is still more pungent than the smell." He took a proper sniff and, containing the smoke in his lungs, bent to place spit-damp baton tip to Fide's lips.

As was to be expected there were grimaces and paroxysms—none so violent Ggau wished to forbid further experiment—but Fide was a determined fellow. Before baton was fully consumed he had mostly mastered the art. "*Friendly, floaty, dreamy,* you told me long ago," he said hoarsely. "I'm relatively friendly to be-gin with. Floaty and dreamy?"

"Some moments more. Here, you'll lean on me." Ggau rear-ranged them comfortably.

Fide toyed with a long crimped lock of Ggau's hair. "One can-not but wonder," he mused, "how the notion of it first occurred."

"One supposes it's no more peculiar than the notion of cooking one's meat."

"Hmm-hah. A branch fallen into the cooking fire which made the savages crouched around it happy so they learned to repeat and eventually perfect the experience."

"Some such circumstance, I expect."

"It is exceptionally pleasant, Ggau, to feel you beside me all large and warm and to hear the thump-thumping of your heart. Although my throat is raw."

"Lovely Fide," said Ggau tenderly, "you are beginning to float."

"Am I? How intriguing. Will we return to our previous dis-course?"

"Auw!" Clickety-clack. "Yes, we must. I wasn't called back to town all winter. It isn't winter as you'll have known in Chuy, un-derstand. Frost rarely, snow never. Rain. There was a good deal to do. I had to grind a new edge onto the cutlass. Da grows 'leaf as well as vine and puts a few fields to wheat when the vines aren't requiring constant care, a special wheat, not for bread but noo-dles."

"*New*," said Fide, dubious. "*Dulls.*"

"Fide! You cannot tell me you've never eaten noodles!"

"Not under that ridiculous name at any rate, I assure you."

"We shall visit Rambertam's directly we make landfall at Yn! In a sauce of cream, wine, mushrooms, aged cheese—sheer bliss in the mouth. With the first fair days of spring arrived a visitor to Da's, a stranger, a foreigner, with a letter from Mother, a bundle of staves and a brace of excellent swords strapped behind her saddle. Mother had hired me a teacher.

"She had two gems of the Steel Conservatory, Noaxtes did. Thesthiri, of course. A jolly woman but stubborn and opinionated. No single-edged weapon met her approval, a mariner's battered cutlass least of all. The blade she'd brought for me was too small, for I'd become a great lunk already and still growing fast, but she had me learn it anyway, trading off with her own, which was too large the first months. Unless Da's had it reforged for plowshare or scythe I've still got that first one, in a chest with the damn cutlass.

"I was learning, Fide, I was being taught! Noaxtes was brutal in her expectations and demands but unstinting in her praise. After half a year I was permitted to visit the swordsmith to choose a blade that fit. She smacked my first choice down, of course: too fancy. *Not weapon but ornament,* she said, *for a foppish toady at court.* The second choice I outgrew in a matter of months, though it wasn't replaced immediately. Before the dinner for my fourteenth birthday she said, *I could teach you more but doubtless just pass on my own bad habits. I'll advise your mother to have you enrolled at the conservatory.*"

"Ggau—all this time, honoring your vow, you'd never cut your hair? And nobody remarked upon it? It's customary in the islands, you said, for men to go cropped."

Ggau shifted comfortably. "Yes, that eccentricity nearly as conspicuous as my coloring. Well, if they wouldn't know better I might say it was a custom of warriors in Mother's country. To others I said the weight on my neck and tension on my scalp helped me concentrate, or no more than that I liked it. Still others I simply glared down."

"Your father, Ggau. Your *mother.*"

"Remarkably, no word was ever spoken."

Fide's belly grumbled. "What's that?" Irritated, he slapped it. "Be still."

"Hunger," said Ggau contentedly, "is a frequent consequence of sniffing 'leaf. How fortunate I anticipated it."

"You did! I remember." Scrambled to his feet, Fide appeared startled by the ferocious fit of stretching and yawning that took him. Done, he found the plate, stuffed a wedge of cheese into his mouth, gathered a fistful of sausage, stretched again. "Ggau! My body is requiring me to move it about. Is this also a consequence of sniffing? Will you walk with me a bit, just back and forth?"

Still reclined, Ggau stretched himself, unkinking his toes. "Allow me just to watch a moment. To see you active after so long ill fills my heart."

Tranquil, he watched Fide stride the five paces from rail to rail and back, munching sausage. "I'm still listening," Fide said.

"Ah, yes. You're not to think it was all swords and staves during Noaxtes's residence. There were chores. I learned to cook."

"Cook!" Fide swung about in astonishment.

"You'll be well enough fed with me. And I read books. Not the love stories you seem to have favored. Adventure stories and traveler's tales and history. Was then I learned my grandda's country was Daewen. You said you knew nothing about Daewen except a reputation for banditry? Seems that's essentially all there was till a hundred years ago or so. A myriad of warlike little clans in their little valleys, raiding each other and plaguing merchants on the Western Road. Then, in the course of not much more than a year, a single poor clan out of the northernmost reaches of the Kikiaddredaes forced all the others to submit. That was Grandda's clan, Garrow. But they didn't do it by themselves."

"The sorcerer." Not a question.

"The sorcerer," Ggau agreed grimly. "Appeared out of nowhere and announced himself as *Garrow's weapon*. I can't know, of course, but imagine it was his notion rather than any Garrow's to forge up a nation out of the quarrelsome clans."

Fide had halted again. "Sorcerers don't *do* that, though, hire themselves out, get involved in ordinary folk's affairs. They're not interested in us, they don't care. What's a *nation* to somebody who can bend the Land Below the Land to make…Fri's beacon? The Fruiting Bridge. Who'll live as near to forever as makes no difference."

"It seems this sorcerer is exceptional in that regard. Calls himself O, by the way."

Fide gnawed a slice of sausage and grumbled, "Ludicrous. More preposterous than *noodles*. Jumped-up witch."

Ggau contemplated. "It's a possibility, I suppose, but makes no difference. Some of the things he's said to have done—I've never heard of a witch capable of such feats. And in my understanding and observation witches age in the normal way at the normal rate. O's said not to have aged a day since his first appearance."

"I don't like it," said Fide, and went back to pacing.

After a moment Ggau said, "It is certainly wonderful to see you so full of vigor," half-addressing a Meffer-niggle in his mind, "but I beg you, my Fide, don't overtire yourself."

"Tired! Just now I don't know what *tired* is. All tingly and glowing and alive." Abruptly Fide cast a dark look Ggau's way. "It's the 'leaf, lying to me."

Sitting up, Ggau held out both hands. "Some people it takes that way. I'd be reassured if you lay down again and let me hold you."

Fide's eyes narrowed, then widened. "An invitation I'd be a fool to decline." But he paused first to fiddle at his shirt buttons and strip it off. "Warm, too."

Tell him 'leaf makes some amorous? But he wishes *to be amorous. As do I so wish him fully capable of it. If it will aid his confidence to be aided—*

Ggau's thought was interrupted by fingers that had bypassed his own plucking at his shirt. "You must undress as well," said Fide with the gravity of a child. "I like the feel of your skin on mine far better than linen."

"It is," said Ggau agreeably, sitting up to sling off jerkin first, "as you say, a warm night," then discovered Fide kneeling between his outspread legs was stark naked. A pang made him swallow: Fide's loveliness, the implicit power in limbs and torso, his vulnerability. "Everything?" Ggau asked, his voice quavering high.

"Of course everything."

Lifting his hands to Fide's elbows, Ggau murmured, "You must give me space a moment then," pulled up his legs, stood.

Breeches momently manacled his ankles but he still wore smalls and open shirt. Palms brushed his shins against leg hair's growth pattern, continued higher. "You are so very...much, my Ggau. Handsome Ggau. I—I feel a fancy."

Benign, Ggau peered down. Fide's cheeks and chest flushed pink, eclipsing freckles and rivaling the vividness of his beard, but he continued brazenly. "I warn you, I've only read about it but I understand it's pleasurable for both parties."

"You intrigue me."

Fide licked his lips. When it came, his voice was not as steady as perhaps he wished it to sound. "Handsome Ggau, may I taste your handsome ass?"

In an instant Ggau's cock came up hard in his smalls and his head went light.

"Don't need a working prick for that, I think."

Inhaling painfully, Ggau saw, and exhaled. He sank to his haunches. "It has escaped your attention," he said very happily as he closed a fist around Fide's stiffness, "yet it stands up to be admired."

Gazing into Ggau's eyes, slowly Fide said, "Astonishing. My request stands as well." His face was still heavily flushed.

"Your request delights me." Concerned, Ggau lifted his free hand to cup one hot cheek. "Is there a verb a thousand-fold more powerful than *delight*? But, Fide, still—a moment. A moment. May I kiss your lovely lips?"

Turning his head pettishly aside, Fide muttered, "You fear I'll do it badly."

"It cannot be done badly. No man's asshole will not welcome lips and tongue upon it. Only, Fide, courageous Fide, not every owner of lips and tongue enjoys pleasuring an asshole. Some find the notion shocking or repulsive."

Stoutly, Fide replied, "I find it extremely shocking. Ggau, how can I know if you won't allow me to try?"

"Nothing is forbidden. I forbid you nothing. As if I ever could. Fide, my asshole is all spasms of anticipation. My prick is flooding my smalls with anticipation."

"Take them off."

"A moment more of delicious suspense. Two moments. I do dearly wish to kiss your mouth. Please."

Half sullen, half abandoned, Fide was upon him in an instant with wrestler's prowess, knocking him flat on his back into a cloud of billowing hair. A bluster of passionate kisses lasted a moment more than a moment, then Fide was kneeling again between his bent-up legs, ripping at the drawstring of sodden smalls.

"Fide...if you've only read about it, nobody's ever kissed *you* there?"

"No."

"I find *that* shocking. Fide—"

"Be *still*, Ggau. I anxiously await experiencing these fabled delights myself when you return the favor but I *will* go first."

Ggau surrendered. Losing patience, Fide ripped his smalls apart at the seams and tossed the rags aside. Breeches-manacles were similarly dispensed with, if without ripping. Fide's face was intent, serious. "On your knees or on your shoulders? My research indicates either provides a propitious angle."

"Please," said Ggau feebly, "shoulders. So I may watch."

"Ggau," said Fide, hoisting his hips into the air, "you are so good to me. You wish to watch—auw, your wish excites me."

Muzzy-headed Ggau doubted Fide could feel as excited as he did. Flailing, he grasped his own calves, rocked his ass higher, wider. His cock dribbled onto his sternum. Fide's face appeared between his thighs, expectant, peaceful. He bent at the shoulders, eyes on Ggau's, and bristled his bearded chin from Ggau's balls back along that ribbon of tender, reactive skin, pathway to the twitching asshole. Ggau flinched, flinched again when bristle-brush scoured it with circular movements longer than he felt he could endure. He endured. In extremity, he blinked his eyes shut, shot them open again. No more was to be seen than scalp, forehead, brows, all blazing like a sunset between the dark peninsulas of his own thighs.

Fide went slowly but without hesitation: curiously. He could not possibly be repulsed. Closed-lip kisses around the rim. Dribbles of spit. Tongue tip lapping—wetting down, Ggau imagined, the surrounding hair and expertly polishing it out of the way. Ggau had had amateurs snuffling his trench as well as greedy veterans: as he'd told Fide, it was all good. The asshole liked to be teased in any number of ways, welcomed all manner of sensation. None of those men had been Fide. Possibly one or another had *cared*, but Ggau hadn't. Humming, Fide kissed deeply, burrowed his tongue. Tantalized, stubborn muscle began to relax. Ggau whimpered. Strong hands bruised his hips, holding him up and wide, preventing him flying away.

Ggau gibbered. Once, or more than once, he caught sight of Fide's magical wide blue eyes at an impossible distance below raised eyebrows and furrowed forehead, weighing his reactions.

"You may," mewled Ggau, "please, whenever you like, please, you may give me your cock."

His asshole flinched shut when Fide removed his mouth. Stern eyes between trembling thighs pierced. "No," Fide said.

"Please. Why?"

"First, we have no oil at hand. Second, I choose not to." A cruelly desirous smirk. "Release your legs, Ggau, and let me lay you flat. I'll sit on your chest and come in your beard."

"Oh!"

"And then it will please me for you to do likewise."

Curled up on his side, Fide lay with his head on Ggau's belly. He might be contemplating Ggau's wrung-out prick, might be dozing. *He is well*, exulted wrung-out Ggau, *he is well, he is well. ...At any rate, well enough to harden up and to shoot magnificently. Such a gift. Such an inexplicable gift. If it won't happen again for another month, I am satisfied.*

Not dozing. "Ggau," Fide murmured, voice low, sated, "you are inordinately kind and good to me."

Flabbergasted, Ggau reared up on his elbows. "*I* am good to *you*?"

Fide would have none of it. He gave Ggau's thigh a little smack. "We were distracted," he said, untroubled.

"We were." *How well we were.*

"You have further to tell me. We have more to discuss."

"We do, yes, I'm afraid."

"But I find myself weary now." Rolling over, he smiled tenderly at Ggau's alarm, swooped an arm up high and a finger down to Ggau's lips, like bee to blossom. "Not the weariness of illness. Of healthy exertion and the natural aftermath of coming. May I sleep a while?"

Ggau felt passionately certain: "You must."

"Will you promise not to chop off your hair while I sleep?"

Ggau hesitated.

"You mustn't hesitate."

"It's not that! There, just at your hairline. I see a forlorn dribble of come I wish to lick up."

"*Kholtenggau.*" Stern. Warning.

"On the promise of your cock in my ass, I solemnly swear."

Fide smiled with great lazy charm. "No, my Ggau, I won't accept that oath just yet. On the promise of your tongue on *my* asshole."

"You are my master in all things. I swear joyfully."

Kiss

Steve Berman

Without air-conditioning, the temperature inside the car racing down the highway felt twenty degrees hotter than the surrounding desert. Beneath the sweaty t-shirt he wore, Mike could feel his back sliding against the seat. His roommate sat behind the wheel with one arm out the window catching the breeze. Blond, shirtless, and tan, eyes concealed behind mirrored sunglasses, Ryan did not seem the least bit diminished by the heat.

"Do you think Tom's a top or a bottom?" he asked, glancing over at Mike.

Tom was supposed to be one of the features at tonight's party. A junior with hopefully more than a 4.0 average. Maybe seven inches. "Does it matter?" Mike had known Ryan to convince the most adamant top to beg with his knees up around his ears.

Ryan grinned, his smile perfect except for a chipped front tooth. He told everyone it had been a skateboarding injury from years back. After several shots of tequila though, Ryan confided that during winter break an ex had hit his face with a fridge door.

He'd met Ryan in their freshman year at U of A. Both shared the same floor of the dorm but separate rooms to start. Then Ryan's roommate had told the RA he wouldn't share space with a faggot. Mike grew up with a pair of "aunts" that helped raise him, so he had no problem volunteering to switch rooms.

Their first kiss had happened while sitting on the floor. Ryan had a few friends over to share some of Canada's finest. Mike turned and saw Ryan waiting for him with the lit end of the blunt in his mouth. He leaned in and touched lips with Ryan, opening his mouth a moment later. THC-laced smoke linked them. Ryan's fingers tapped an echo of the rising heartbeat against the back of his neck.

Mike had never before tasted boy or drug and found the two flavors to his liking.

Ryan swerved the car to avoid the flattened carcass of a rabbit lying in the middle of the road.

"Chupacabra."

"Huh?" Mike glanced over his shoulder at the road behind him.

"That's what killed the rabbit." Ryan lifted his gaze to the rear-view mirror.

"Looked like a Goodyear going sixty-five was to blame." "Nope, the chupacabra," Ryan said. "What the hell is that?" Mike peeled his back from the car seat. "The Mexican goat-sucker." Mike looked at Ryan, expecting to see a stupid grin. The handsome face didn't disappoint him. "Is that like a Dirty Sanchez?" "How come I'm from California and I've heard of it?" Mike shrugged. Now and then he felt diminished being around Ryan. "Like every boy from Tucson has." "They're aliens." "Wait, I thought you said they're Mexicans. How can they be both?" "Maybe they're illegal aliens?"

"That's so bad," Mike said with a groan. "They're supposed to be these creatures that drain the blood from animals." Ryan dropped his voice low, as if to be spooky. "People, too, on occasion. They look like spiny little gray men with tongues like a frog, 'cept that's how they drink, like through a straw."

"Right." Mike stared out into the desert. It looked so empty. Lonely was the word that came to mind. "So you've bought from this guy before, right?" "Yeah." Ryan looked away from the road for a moment to pick through jewel cases in the bin between the seats. "Here, the Redcaps. Track four." He slid the CD into the dashboard. Harsh lyrics that blended with industrial beat filled the car. Ryan tapped the wheel with his slender fingertips in time to the music. "Cruz deals the best shit. Tonight's party will be made by what we bring back." "Cool," Mike said though he didn't want to rush their return to campus. At the party, he'd have to compete for Ryan's attention. Ryan tapped the brake pedal once before turning onto a dirt side road. Clouds of reddish dust blew from around the tires. "Where do you know about all this shit?"

"What, the peyote? Mescalito?" A chuckling Ryan shook his head. "My brother was kicked out of pharmacy school." Mike knew that real life had worse things than bogeymen. Envy. Want. Loneliness. These sudden and new sensations frightened him— not superstition. "No, the chuba..."

"Chup-acabra. That's from Alvaro." "I thought you said this guy's name is Cruz." Ryan nodded. "Alvaro was this kid I met back in high school. Tutored me in Spanish. Was the first uncut cock I ever saw." Mike laughed, trying not to think how long it had taken him to lose his virginity. The event, much fumbling in the back of the girl's Jeep, was not worth bragging. Ryan always had better stories than he could muster. "Did you get an 'A' on the tests?" "B minus. Just to make sure I got weekly visits. Still, I was his best mayate pupil."

"Just never tell me exactly how many guys you've done. I don't want to be scared."

"Aww, poor Mikey." Ryan's tone stung. "Maybe tonight you can work on catching up to me." They'd slept together a few times after becoming roommates. But Ryan's eye and mouth wandered a lot, and Mike had no choice but to graduate to "best friend" when it was clear that being boyfriend wasn't an option. The last time they'd done anything was after Jell-O shots. They'd woken up in bed together, mostly clothed, and sipped water from a bottle together to rehydrate. Mike had spilled some on his chest and a playful Ryan dribbled more onto Mike's boxers. From there, the hangovers had been forgotten. Ryan slowed down on the dirt road and the car felt the bumps. After twenty minutes, an eyesore broke the ennui of the desert landscape: a battered trailer surrounded by scarred lawn furniture. A fake deer with bleached and broken antlers guarded the door. An old Ford pickup truck, hood flipped open, rested unhitched nearby. Ryan pulled up beside the trailer. He craned his neck out the open window and called out. "¡Oye ese! ¿Que hay de nuevo?"

Moments later the trailer door popped open. Squinting at the sun from the darkness of the interior, a dusky skinned, stout man stepped out. His pitch-black hair was pulled back in a ponytail. Shirtless, his chest was a blend of curved muscle and fat around his stomach, a torso in transition from football player bulk to couch potato. "Hola." Ryan grinned at Mike. "Get ready for some of the best shit you'll ever taste," he said as he got out of the car. "Cruz," he called out and met the dealer with a hand slap. "Baja, you brought a friend." Cruz looked Mike over from top to bottom, while rubbing the scruff along his neck. "Baja?" Mike worried the two had once played around. "Heh, I call him that," Cruz said, playfully batting at Ryan's chest. "He's all Californian. So you have money?" Ryan pulled a wad of folded bills from a pocket of his cargo shorts. Cruz smiled. "Good. Come inside."

The trailer was dim and much too warm. Mike grimaced at the rank blend of sweat, marijuana smoke, and fried sausage. Cruz led them to the left and back before collapsing on the unmade bed, a stained mattress peeking through tangled sheets, and reaching for shoeboxes scattered along a shelf.

"Mescalito," Cruz said and yawned as he took down one box. Mike glanced inside at the plastic bag filled with what looked like a bunch of dried little turds. Ryan reached in took out one of the small buttons. "It's the top of a local cactus." He popped it into his mouth then grimaced as he chewed. Mike did the same. The taste was hot and bitter, leaving his tongue and mouth numb. "Ugh, and to think I'm wasting my time majoring in history." Ryan smirked. "That shit's tradition to the natives. More than the chupacabra."

"Goat-sucker?" Cruz barked a laugh. "Here, the only thing good for sucking is this." Cruz grabbed the crotch of his cut-offs and squeezed the outline of his cock. Mike doubted the dealer wore any underwear.

Cruz next rummaged and found a fat joint that he lit on the trailer's burner. He took a deep hit then held it out to Ryan. "¿Grilla, Baja?" "When do I ever say no?" Ryan took several deep hits, refreshing the stink in the air, before passing it to Mike.

The pot was strong, stronger than he ever had, though maybe it was 'cause of the peyote button he had just swallowed. His stomach felt queasy. He passed the joint back to Cruz who smirked at both of them.

"I can give you some of this, for free...only..."

"Only what?" Mike asked.

"Only ir a rechinar la cama."

Ryan laughed.

"What does that mean?" Mike asked.

Ryan stepped close to his roommate. He slipped his arms around Mike's neck and lightly kissed him, making him blush. "He wants to fuck around."

Mike stared at Cruz, who began unbuttoning his shorts. The trail of dark hair began around his stomach and got thicker the lower it went. "I...I..."

"Don't worry 'bout it, Mikey," Ryan giggled. "I go through this all the time with Cruz. You don't have to join in."

Ryan turned back to Cruz and took the joint from the dealer's mouth. He took one last hit and then passed it to Mike, who watched as his best friend slipped his shorts off.

Mike couldn't stay to watch. He wouldn't. The inside of the trailer felt blistering hot and his head throbbed, like too much blood circulated around his temples. He stumbled outside, trying not to think of them together.

The setting sun was not the right color. It took him a moment staring at the sunset to realize the red had changed to a purplish hue, like the desert at midnight. He stood there, trying not to eavesdrop on the loud springs complaining and the grunts and groans. When he heard Cruz yell out, "Chupame la polla," Mike moved further away from the trailer, his eyes never straying from the horizon.

Something moved out there. The rocks maybe. They looked taller, more angular. No, something definitely shifted near the sunset. A shape, scuttling over the desert.

He watched it move until he felt so sick from the colors and the heat in his stomach that he leaned over and vomited on the hard soil. A bit of his lunch stained his sandals and feet.

When he looked back up the nearby ceramic deer seemed ten feet tall and frowned down at him. A little frightened, he looked away. The shape was closer. It must move quickly when he wasn't watching. He could make it out now. A hunched-over figure. Maybe. It looked dark against all the colors that had sprung up on the desert. It crawled over the outcroppings, now and then leaping towards him.

Mike watched it twitch and scamper, now some fifty feet off. He could see the failing light shine off large black eyes staring at him. The thing's outline wavered, for a moment shifting to become just a fractal of the landscape's kaleidoscope, before returning. Only this time he could see spines raised along the thing's back.

Damn. Mike shuffled forward, stepping into a ditch and twisting his ankle. It took far too long for the pain to reach his head and make him look down. Each toe had become stretched to amazing proportions. He wiggled them and marveled at how they could go on for miles.

The deer began laughing at him. It had Ryan's voice.

When he glanced up the spiny thing was close. For a moment, its stare shifted to the same green hue as his roommate's eyes. From its slack mouth unfurled a long tongue. Instinctively, Mike leaned in closer.

The very end of the imagined—he knew it had to be imagined—chupacabra's tongue lifted towards his face. The puckered tip had a glistening dew drop. Mike half-closed his eyes and licked his lips, remembering that kiss with Ryan. It had been smoky, tickling the back of his throat, and not fading as the drug flowed through his lungs. Mike had never wanted it to end, but it had. He hoped this new kiss, however how delusional, promised more than his first.

Carousel

Nelson Stanley

I watch you ride.

Up and down, up and down, easy practiced rhythm. My eyes pass over your coat-hanger shoulders, down the V of your torso, following the beads of sweat turning your thick hair to a mop. As you ride you laugh, head tossed back: long fine muscles of your forearms, the definition of your lats, stand out in relief. Lights wheel across the night, blurred to chrysanthemum shards. The air reeks of hydraulic oil and burnt sugar. I can still taste you—the sour musk of your arse, bitter ketones of your sweat, sweet alkali burn of your come—on my tongue.

The last joint we shared dangles at ease in my lips, half-forgotten. I light it up and take the last hit, feel the scrape against my lungs, the warmth that slips from cell-to-cell until my body seems filled with hot sweet smoke, like my lungs have leaked inside and it's seeped out of them into every extremity of my body. Time diffuses across my nerve endings like a drop of oil. As if from far away, as if with someone else's eyes, I look down: I'm getting hard again.

Above the noise of the hydraulics, Celine Dion caterwauls from hidden speakers: her heart will go on.

I watch you ride, and wonder if mine might burst.

*I*grew up in a desperately sad little seaside town in southern England, a place the Nazis didn't so much forget to bomb as didn't think warranted the expenditure of ammunition. It basically had two places to deal: a pier (more on that, later) and a "leisure park", a half-out-of-town wasteland built on a literal bit of waste land, where a shitty nightclub nestled in the lee of a dozen plastic chain stores and a four-screen cinema that seemed to show nothing but fucking Adam Sandler flicks, one after the other.

I'd move a bit there, to kids too young to get fucked-up in pubs or those like me who preferred the herb and were too awkward for a scene. Every weekend—or on weekdays, when the sun went down and the workaday people left, as the orange floodlights began to glimmer in the gloam—knots of boys and girls huddling in their hoodies or under baseball caps would sprout under the leaking awnings of the chain stores. Clouds of sweet hash smoke would billow as they crowded in corners and behind the ornamental bushes, getting fucked-up and fucking each other while gangsta rap, hxc and drum'n'bass pumped out of the endlessly circling hatchbacks in the car park. Boy-racers released from their day-jobs would blat it hard up to the speed-bumps then brake so heavily you'd think their front spoilers would plough up the tarmac, then squeal off to practice their doughnuts and handbrake turns in their bazzed-up Escorts and Corsas, leaving a hint of sinsemilla to sweeten the exhaust smoke.

A good weekend I could move half a nine-bar of plasticky soap—dry, brown, hard like a shit that had been in your colon for days, studded with little lumps of cling-film that'd fizzle when you heated it, a tell-tale sign that what you were smoking started life as the crap they swept off the floor—every weekend there, to those who couldn't afford ten quid a gramme for hydro from the boy-racers or were too scared to brave the macho bullshit that went hand-in-hand in dealing with them: gaggles of young scared-looking townie girls in skirts like belts, anxious knots of sweet little queers chewing on their new lip-or-tongue piercings, box-fresh bulldykes in lumberjack shirts with shaved heads and one long shock of hair dyed violent neon; the freaks, the loners, outcasts from something they'd never wanted to join in with in the first place. People like me.

There wasn't any security that I ever bumped in to, but occasionally the place would sicken: there was only so often I could watch the boy-racers offer some thirteen-year-old girl a discount on a baggie if they'd slip into the passenger bucket seat. Or, like they did the day I'm gonna tell you about, watching them snatch the notes out of a skinny little goth's hand and burn off in a haze of fat low-profiles, then slow and wait for the kiddie to trot dutifully after them before revving up and speeding off again. If the boy was lucky then they might get to scrabble for an underweight zip-lock flung out of a window; if not, they'd stand there all defeated watching the rear end shimmy as the boy-racer zoomed away.

If they were *really* unlucky, like that day in late summer, they'd catch up with the car, and then there'd be a screech of brakes followed by a swiftly-administered kicking for leaving paw-prints over a dodgily bolted-on rear spoiler.

I watched the boy fall, checked I had both my mobiles on me, then turned away and caught the bus across town, to the seaside, my hoodie pockets stuffed full of carefully weighed-up baggies, to where the comically old-fashioned pier stuck out into the sea like an erection at a family gathering.

The world revolves, slow churn in the warm night air. The lights. The music.

Baby, you make the whole fucking world spin.

If I had the words, my love, I'd tell you what you mean to me, I'd freeze this moment in time and list all the sensations you spark across my nerve-endings. If I had the words, I'd spin it out in a rush, a torrent, a pulsing spasm: the way the feeling builds when you've been so expertly teasing me—rising up through me in a glistening pulse that seems to coalesce in a tight throbbing knot at the base of my balls then rises and explodes out of me in a judder, a quivering cadence that leaves me in a tiny mess of aftershocks that strobe through me, from my fingers to my toes, a feeling so intense in the end of my cock I swear I can feel my piss-hole quiver. The feeling that fills my heart as you lick me clean and then look up at me, waggle your eyebrows, flash me a lop-sided grin that turns my knees to water and fills my cock with blood.

I might tell you something like that. But I don't have the words. I don't have words. You roll another joint on my chest, somewhat discomfited in this task by my sweat, reach down to fondle my balls. The night is warm and the stars are on the water that laps softly at the edge of hearing. You pull your hoodie up over me as I start to shiver.

"You are the only person I've ever met who could skin up one-handed," I burble, and you smile as you lick the j shut and light up.

You take a hit, hold it and—releasing me—move up over my chest to exhale into my mouth, filling my lungs with langour even as your other hand goes to my groin again. We are made of sensation, made of feeling, of light and shade. We are made of heat and smoke. You finish shotgunning into my mouth and nibble me, tugging at my skin like the munchies have got too much to bear, chasing the shivers down my clavicle, my sternum, your breath so light on my stomach—hint of divine prickling from your stubble, just coming through—so warm, then your tongue traces my belly-button and then the periphery of my pubes before plunging into the secret fissures between my balls and my thigh. I gasp and your tongue moves lower, an animal snuffling out something secret from a crevice, your tongue firm and delicate on my arsehole, shivers of pleasure floating through me.

You pull back, take a hit, let it out slow so that you're wreathed in smoke. I'm hard again and you lick it until I'm good and wet, then straddle me, ease yourself down on to me.

I love to watch you ride. I watch you ride.

There was a desperately sad little funfair set up at the end of the pier, in front of the Pavilion—a sort of low-capacity gig venue where mildly racist post-vaudeville light entertainment acts went to die. I hung about on the outskirts of the fair for a while, mingling with the grotesques slipping on the greasy planking, the old people and the crazies, the caterwauling children and harried parents pulling candy-floss out of their hair. A lot of bad music clashed, and people pressed tight around me. I sparked the emergency bifter I kept in my hoodie (a fat double-skinner stuffed with pale Moroccan pollen that crumbled like powdered gold) and pushed through the crowds, past a dozen identical striped tourist-bait stalls, past grim takeaways flogging fish and chips with a uniquely soapy aftertaste and unidentifiable bits of shellfish like congealed snot in polystyrene punnets.

I paused amidst the looped circus music coming out of a Chair-o-Plane that looked like it'd seen better days, half the neon bulbs blown and the thick reek of hydraulic grease mingling with the screams of the victims as they sailed past overhead. It was great, stoned as I was: the coloured lights, the knots of people crowding between the coconut shy and the "hook the plastic fish and win a prize" stalls. The chemical smell of candy-floss and the deep nauseating stink of frying fishy things.

Just as I felt the hit—just as my spit went sour with that familiar alkali, earthy tang, just as the world went soft around the edges—a gap opened in the mass of people in front of me. Then:

a constellation of stars across my vision, wheeling, rising and fall-ing. I blinked. My eyes were filled with rococo red-and-gold, and the whoops and shrieks of people bled into Celine Dion's voice squalling out on a midst of soft rock that, right at that minute, I didn't mind at all (it *was* really good hash).

As my eyes adjusted to my new reality the music died, seeping back into the cracks in the world. I was standing in front of the most beautiful old carousel, a merry-go-round that looked like it had staggered from some Victorian children's fantasy, a scarlet and aureate wedding-cake slowing to a crawl. I stood transfixed, drinking in the laughter as happy people prepared to descend from the carved wooden horses that were frozen forever mid-gal-lop, spitted on the barley-twist poles. It filled me with the sense of something I couldn't quite name, a sense of beautiful loss, a nostalgia for something that I couldn't articulate.

As it stopped and the people got off—pushing against the queue of people waiting to get on, held back by a hard-faced woman in overalls with a do-rag, puffing on a Marlboro—I saw a guy moving out from the machinery in the centre and out amongst the horses, eyes narrowed, checking stuff before the ride could go again. He was tall and lean, shaggy hair, oil-stained T-shirt and jeans. I was struck by the way he was going over the carousel, intimate and serious with the secrets of the pleasure-machine, absorbed in his work, making sure this beautiful thing ran clean and true before the noisy crowd could get onboard again. As if feeling my eyes on him he stopped suddenly and straightened up, eyes scanning the crowd. Crazy as it was—stoned as I was—I knew he was looking at me, straight at me, straight through me. I felt singled out, like the rush and crush of people around me had suddenly recoiled away from me, leaving me stranded under that gaze. The sun be-gan to dip towards the horizon and then The Fear really hit me.

You know it. We've all been there. Most of us have stumbled into this state at about two a.m. in a convenience store and there's a new guy behind the counter, a guy you don't recognise, you get spooked so you walk into a rack of crisps or nearly out-of-date chocolates and all the eyes in the room not fixed on you already just have to turn your way…

Try that at a crowded fun-fair on a shitty little pier as the sun goes down on a dog-day of summer, while the impassive, unknowable stare of a beautiful man singles you out of a crowd.

So, cupping the joint expertly in my hand, I split.

I get on my knees in front of you, take you in my mouth, tongue finding the groove on the underside of your frenulum, my hands grasping the firmness of your arse, pulling you on to me, in to me.

Your half-erect cock makes contact with the back of my mouth, making me gag a little. I pull back, and you leave a trail of spit and pre-come that drips over my chin. I take your length in my hand and run my hands up and down you as I work your head with my whole mouth, folding my lips back over my teeth while I suck on you, gently at first, then faster, faster, going deeper, deeper, lapping at your pre-come with my tongue. The wooden decking of the pier is slimy on my knees, but I don't care, I don't care. The smell of the sea, the noise of the waves, the gloaming, you above me, naked and beautiful, head thrown back, one thick vein standing out on your ever-swelling cock. The thickness of you; the taste of you, the smell of sweat and oil and wood and the sea. I can get both hands around you now, but I let the one nearest me fall away and stretch my mouth wide and gulp you down, surprising myself by the fierceness of my desire, my own cock rigid against my stomach, deeper, deeper into my mouth, until you make the sweetest noise—somewhere between an exhalation and a groan, a noise from somewhere deep inside—and with a shudder that seems to shake the earth you pour yourself down my throat, all heat and salt.

Both hands then, round my face. Your work-rough hands are so gentle on my face, like I wasn't just a small-town pot dealer, like I wasn't just another fuck-up: you hold me like I was worth something, like I was something beautiful and fragile, like I was something rare and wondrous, and languid and slow and just a tiny bit sad, and you gently tilt my chin up until I meet your eyes, the same sad green as the sea.

"Fuck me," you whisper.

I had a bolt-hole. There were big bits of checker-plate bolted to the sides of the pier, twenty feet below the main concourse, a few feet above the water, like something attached to an oil rig. They were used as fishing platforms; now, in the dying afternoon and with the fair in full-swing they were empty, rusting slowly in the sea-salt air, shat upon by gulls. I wheeled and jostled through the laughing people, the candy-floss and the noise, nipped over the chained-up gate and down the rickety metal staircase. Hand on the flaking rail I made my way down to the fishing platforms, away from the fair, to the comfort of the huge concrete stanchions arranged in an elaborate criss-cross pattern, uprights disappearing down into the dark water.

I made myself comfortable, just out the wind, sitting down against the railing, legs dangling over the side. I watched the waves, the gulls dipping and wheeling low over the water. I felt The Fear recede even as the sounds of the fair receded, as if being sucked out by the water churning a few feet below. I sat there for a while, the sunlight bleeding from gold to rose, kicking my heels. I re-lit my spliff, took a big lungful, held it.

"Mind if I join you?"

I jumped so hard I nearly dropped my smoke. Convulsing, coughing, I turned around, trying not to fall into the sea.

He walked forward, now in an oversized hoodie and blue jeans. My hand clenched the baggies in my pocket, little lumps of certainty and comfort divided into precise fractions of an ounce. The gulls screamed overhead.

"Gotta light?" he said, his voice easy, a smile playing across his full lips.

I teetered on the edge of turning away, of pushing past and running back up the steps and finding somewhere else to get mashed. I could've gone back to the leisure park, or gone home to the council house where Mum would be sipping grey tea and watching gameshows, another evening staring blindly at a wash of light in a darkened room, munching on her digestive biscuits.

"Sure," I said.

I dug the lighter out of my pocket, and tried to get my facial muscles to obey me and smile, and moved towards him, weaving slightly across the checker-plate. Now I could see him clearer I could see he was a boy about my age, olive skin, heart-shaped face and eyes the colour of a winter afternoon at the seaside, and he took the lighter from my hand and sparked up half a joint he had cupped in his hand the whole time.

He flashed me a smile, which made my knees give just a little, and he sat down next to me. I sparked mine and in companionable silence, we spent a few minutes of the afternoon puff-puff-giving back and forth, while the gulls threatened to dive-bomb us and the waves surged at the uprights. After a few tokes I offered him my smoke, and he smiled as he swapped mine for his. I admit it: I coughed.

"Nasty fuckin' ditchweed. Sorry. Best you can get, on the road."

I nodded, stared at the foamy sea.

"You on the road a lot?"

"Yeah. I'm with the fair."

"I know." Fighting against the cotton wool in my head, my mouth drying like I had a wad of blotting paper in it. "I...saw you. I mean, the uh, the merry-go-round—"

"Carousel." He took a hit from my joint, nodded appreciatively, swapped back. "He's beauty, isn't he? Over a hundred years old. Used to have panels on it, you know. The carousel. Painted on. Above the poles. Did you ever watch *Mary Poppins*?"

"No," I said. "But I've watched *The Magic Roundabout*."

"Er, yeah. Well, that bit where whatshisname, and the kids, and Mary, they've all gone to this fair, see, and then they get on the carousel, and it goes faster and faster, and they're having such a good time. And the music gets louder and the carousel keeps going, faster and faster, and the next thing you know they're riding the horses straight off the carousel, I mean it's still spinning but it's like the horses have got loose and the next minute they've broken free and then they're off, riding the horses, they're like real horses, I mean, they've ridden them right off the carousel and then they're going across fields hunting a fox and then they're in a horse race and then—"

He stopped, toked, held it, scrunched up his face, blew smoke out of his nostrils. From above drifted the sounds of people screaming, possibly with pleasure. It was difficult to tell.

"Well," he said after a while, "I fucking hated that film. But I always wanted a horse."

I was mid-toke and couldn't help it, broke into a laugh I tried to disguise as a cough, chanced a quick glance at him but he was still staring at the waves, at something I couldn't see, and he went on, voice gone dreamy from the reminisce or the gear:

"My Dad, my Dad he says we're Travellers, not show-folk, that's what we are, and I used to dream of having a horse, like, a proper Romany horse, a big fucking bay."

"So.... You're what? A Gypsy?"

"Yeah." He took a hit. "We go around, put the fair up. Town to town, like. Always on the drom." He held his hit, exhaled a near-solid plume of smoke upwards, towards the fair. "I don't mind the life. Closest I can get to horses now, you know?"

"I'm scared of horses," I muttered, around a lungful.

"If I'd had one, I'd have looked after it, treated it like a proper grai, plaited its tail and mane with ribbons, I'd've—"

He stopped, wrenched back from childhood equine dreams. He stared at me in something like disbelief, then his face cracked into a lop-sided grin.

"Are you? Really?"

"Yep. Terrified."

"Why?"

"I dunno. Just am. Something about the teeth, maybe."

He laughed, full-throated, head thrown back.

"But horses are lovely, mush! I mean, they're smart. Dogs aren't smart. A dog'll follow you, but it don't know you like a horse knows you."

"If they're so smart," I said, finishing my J and flipping the roach into the roiling sea, "How come they let cunts like us ride them everywhere?"

He took a hit, held it, then stubbed his roach on the checker-plate.

"They're smart *and* tolerant."

"Right."

The wind got up and blew some gulls about. One seemed to hang against the sky, riding the turbulence rolling off the edges of the pier with little flips of its wings, slowly twisting in the current. I rolled up another from my stash, cursing as the wind tore at my papers, but I got it together and sparked it, feeling the harsh scrape on my lungs. As I did I looked over at him a second too long. He was staring at me, slow and even and steady, so I exhaled through my nostrils and hid in the smoke, a Delphic Oracle gone bashful and baked. He reached over and gently pinched the joint from between my fingers. The touch of his skin sent a jolt up through me, pure feeling sparking through the warm sinkhole of my high: I was immediately aware of my balls, the way they were plumbed in to the rest of me, of my cock stirring against my thigh. He smoked quietly, watched me for a while. He went to speak, timed his hit wrong, coughed. I grinned as he thumped himself on the chest and passed it back.

"Good shit."

"I know. My stash."

"Ah. Not for sale, eh?"

I fumbled in the zip-up pocket of my hoodie, fished in the empty baccy packet inside, felt the comforting lump of powdery Moroccan, so different to the glassy wax-henna-fuck-knows-what feel of the shit I sold. I bit off a chunk, reached out and pressed it into his unresisting hand.

"Here. Gratis."

He clenched his hand over it, touching me for just a second too long. I shuffled my legs underneath me, stood up, swaying slightly. The dying sun came out from amidst the clouds. I felt the warm prickle of sweat on my brow, felt a bead go wandering down my spine, tickle in the crack of my arse. I loosened my hoodie.

"I better go," I said. "You gotta get back."

He reached out a hand, long fingers against the leg of my jeans. I felt my cock thicken.

"My dinner break," he said, voice disappearing into the rumble of the surf. "I don't have to get back for another half an hour."

A smile, sweet and slow, started somewhere in his pale green eyes, licked at the edges of his lips, then exploded outwards until it filled my heart, the sky, the world.

I know this is one of those moments where you start making retching noises, and I don't blame you. But that smile probably dried out my fucking acne, and that is how I met the first boy I ever truly loved. Or something like it, anyway. He moved in, all movement gone tectonic from the hash and his mouth found mine, his tongue in my throat and his hands hungry underneath my clothes.

We floated on that fishing platform above the water, braced against the railing, limbs intertwining in a slow liquid congress, need slicking us together. We floated. I felt blood flow into me, lengthen me. Long fingers shucked my jeans: I ran my hands around his snake-hips and he hissed at me, leaned in and flicked his tongue over my lips. I bit him, quickly, savagely, on the side of his neck where the cords stood out, and he thrust his groin at me, forcing me backwards a few paces. I felt his hardness against my leg. I went to touch him, but he pulled my jeans down, hands fumbling; I watched the bundles of hash fall from my pocket, a slow-motion dream as he took me, in his mouth, licking it from the tip to my balls, soft and gentle and insistent. It might've been the hash or he might've been the most practised I've ever had but I came so hard, a rush that came out of me with a howl, head thrown back.

Standing, he kissed me roughly, the taste of my own come tart on my tongue.

"Fuck me," I whispered, but he shook his head.

"I gotta go. But we knock off in a couple of hours. Come back. Tonight."

So I did. And every night the fair was in town, I turned up just before close, a fresh lump of powdery Moroccan in my pocket and lust in my heart.

I slip my tongue inside, taste your secrets, then slide a finger into you, every nerve a tingle, every movement slow like we're underwater, every motion filled with sensation, then my finger moves past the knuckle, deeper, making you convulse then cry out. I straddle you as you straddle the horse, knees clamped around it and arse shoved out over its rump, my free hand on the barley-pole for balance, leaning over your back.

"Ready?"

"Yes. Now. Now..."

Then: tightness clamped around my cock, easy-easy-easy, you wince so I go slow, feeling you clamp but you turn your head and whisper over your shoulder:

"Don't stop."

Slowly, slowly easing into you, and the giggles rush up my throat warm and easy and you cry out, and we ride, we ride, the movement of the horse as it gallops on its pole taking me deeper inside you as the horse ascends pulling you away, only to ease you back down with a gasp, each motion taking me deeper inside you, teasing us both, the polished wood smooth against my balls, heat of you against my chest. Just as the tight grasp of your arse starts its gentle peristalsis, our rhythms matching yet opposite, I pull myself up on the pole and push all the way inside you and we're locked together, riding, up and down and round and round. Celine Dion belts out as you howl and I come, rush of heat and light, whimpering, clinging to you as the carousel slows to its inevitable stop.

*I*t only lasted a week; the fair packed up and moved on.

Though I knew it was coming, I still cried. We were sharing a smoke on the fishing platform.

"I thought we'd have one more night," I sobbed, but he shook his head and touched my cheek, kissed me roughly, then pulled back, stared levelly at me with those sea-green eyes.

"I'm always moving on," he said. "Just how things are. But remember the horses. Remember the lights. Remember the way I made you feel." He brushed my tears away, leaving a smear of oil on my cheek, plucked the joint from my fingers and sucked greedily on it. I felt myself move inside my shorts, blinked away tears, nodded. But I knew it had to be.

Even now, years later, now my belly's spread and I've assumed a more bearish countenance, every time I take a toke, just as that totalising unity of feeling spreads through my bones and the reassuring sweet heaviness grows in my head, I close my eyes and remember: a pair of green eyes, nights slowly revolving under a whirl of flashing lights, two bodies moving languid as a curl of smoke.

One thing's for sure: I'm certainly not scared of horses any more.

Shotgun

John Dumas

*M*att flopped down on his couch after a busy day at the pizza place, his shoes off, his jeans unzipped before his butt hit the stained cushion of the mustard-colored couch he and Scott had found near the dumpster they day he moved in, his battered laptop already playing a video of two guys swapping blowjobs. The plan was porn, stroking, and a joint.

His manager turned a blind eye to his pot smoking since Matt's Fiesta was reliable and Matt gave his manager a good discount on weed or took payment in beer, which Matt couldn't buy for another two years. The unofficial combo of pizza and weed when Matt was working meant for some very loyal and frequent customers, which didn't hurt either.

As his hand slid past his treasure trail, the spiky blond hairs just slightly lighter than the hairs of his head tickled his wrist as he went to fish his dick out of the plaid boxers. It had been a while since Matt had the courage to hook up with anyone, so the porn would have to do.

His iPhone, face down next to the laptop, interrupted him. It wasn't odd for Matt's phone to ring at eleven p.m., usually with someone looking for some late-night pot. He pulled his hand out of his pants and grabbed the phone. When he saw Scott's name on the screen, his first thought was that Scott was inviting him to head out to party. He'd be up for that.

"Smoke me up, bro, Brianna dumped my ass." Scott's ass had been a centerpiece of Matt's jack off fantasies from the first time he saw it framed in a jock strap in the high school locker room.

"Aw, dude, not again?"

Scott spending a few nights over while things cooled off had become so frequent that he no longer asked if he could crash, but went right to suggesting one of their favorite activities.

"Looks like I'll be riding shotgun with you for a bit."

Scott appreciated the occasional lift from Matt, since he didn't have a car himself. Whenever Scott rode along, he would call out "shotgun," to Brianna's annoyance, who would sulk in the back seat. "Matt's my friend, not our chauffeur, do you want to sit up front?" She would just continue looking at her phone or adjusting her makeup. They'd always just laugh since "shotgun" was their private joke, since every time they smoked pot together, Scott would insist on doing a shotgun.

But he wasn't calling for a ride.

It had been a familiar pattern: Scott and Brianna would get together for a couple months, then there's be a fight that had Scott crashing on Matt's sofa for a couple of weeks, they'd get back together, and Matt would get back to fantasizing about his old buddy at a distance. As a result of Scott's frequent sleepovers, their boxers had become inextricably commingled, but Matt deliberately swiped the boxers he had on because he knew they had cradled Scott's body and had been swapped back and forth, making the stains near the fly a joint project.

"Sure, come on over. I was just about to smoke up, anyway." Matt quit the porn and stashed the laptop away, wishing that he had managed to blast out a load before Scott called, since if he was spending the night with Scott, he'd probably have a boner and no opportunity to deal with it.

Scott's temporary residency presented both advantages and disadvantages. He slept in boxers on the battered sofa hastily covered with a sheet and invariably kicked things off in the night giving Matt a view of his morning wood. He wandered about casually nude after showering, permitting Matt to continue the census of the freckles on Scott's firm butt, all fuel for later jack off sessions. Lately, Scott slept over so frequently that wondered if he should just let him keep the spare key, which would piss off Brianna, but she didn't really like him anyway.

Scott walked in with a frown over the red stubble on his chin, but the moment he saw Matt he broke into a crooked grin. "Hey, honey, I'm home!" He set the paper bag stuffed with his clothes onto his skateboard and held out his arms for a hug. Scott's t-shirt and shorts, his uniform for the skateboard shop, hid a taut body that Matt, slender but not as muscular, both desired and envied.

Matt was relieved since all too often Scott would come over anxious and angry, only to end up sobbing when he got buzzed, but this time Scott folded Matt up in a hug, pressed his face to Matt's neck, and mumbled "dude, you are a fucking lifesaver. I totally owe you." One hand slid up and further tousled Matt's dark blond hair.

Matt broke away from the hug, unwilling to let his friend know just how much he enjoyed it, the Scott-induced boner already growing in the purloined boxers. "Hey, you wanted to smoke and I'm ready for you." He had used the time waiting for Scott to roll a joint. He thought briefly of rolling a second, but wanted to gauge Scott's mood first. Fuck that crying-on-the-couch-all-night shit. "Make yourself at home."

The pair plopped down on the couch that Scott had vacated only a few weeks before. Arrayed on the scarred coffee table as if a votive offering were a green lighter, a battered metal ashtray almost denuded of its former purple coating, and the skillfully rolled joint.

Scott folded his hands and intoned, "Thank you, Matt, for the bounty I am about to receive," finishing off with a laugh. "Light that shit up!"

"Be my guest."

Matt's lips hadn't closed before Scott darted forward, snatching up a joint to the click of the lighter. Scott didn't exhale until Matt was sucking the smoke into his own lungs. Scott breathed in again and said, "Fuck, dude, I needed that."

When Matt went to pass the joint back, he surprisingly waved it away. "You gotta hear what she said. She said that I needed a new job, new clothes, and that I need to stop smoking pot. Fuck her." He finally took a drag on the joint, held the smoke in for a bit. "Or unfuck her," laughing at his joke.

They passed the joint back and forth a couple times, then Scott said, "Let's do a shotgun," taking the joint from Matt. Matt kinda hated and loved doing shotguns with Scott, since on one hand Matt had to fight the desire to turn it into a kiss when Scott's lips were so close to his, but on the other hand at least Scott was placing his lips there. He sucked in the smoke, holding it, then blew it into Scott's waiting mouth, only a slim space away from a kiss.

Scott licked his lips. "Your turn," he rasped. When Scott pulled the joint away from Matt, he planted his lips right on Matt's, who was briefly too shocked to remember to suck in the smoke. As the pressure in their mouths decreased, Scott's tongue snaked its way into Matt's mouth. Matt went for it, reciprocated, since if his bud wanted to make out, who was he to complain? Not when it was a jack off fantasy come true, the thing he'd wanted to do so many times and never dared to. Matt took a drag then leaned into Scott, breathing the smoke into him as the tips of their tongues rubbed against each other.

Scott broke the kiss and said, "Fuck yeah, that's how to shot-gun!"

Scott laughed at his joke a bit, then leaned in for another kiss, the joint smoldering in the ashtray. As his tongue explored Matt's mouth, his hands started their own exploration of Matt's body. Matt got in a little exploration of his own before they both decided to stop neglecting the joint, and they smoked, looked at each other, and with a wheezy laugh, kissed, and then smoked some more.

Scott handed the joint to Matt and said, "Dude, you got a boner."

Matt flushed a little at the news that it had been noticed. "Just thinking about stuff. Relaxing."

"S'okay." Scott pulled his shorts tight, showing a bulge running along his inner thigh. "Me too. Gets you horny, doesn't it?"

It wasn't the first time that they had got hard while smoking together, but while Matt had often thought of turning it into a mutual jack-off session, he had never dared make the next move. "Yeah, it does. Real horny."

"And it looks like you got a nice one there." Scott reached over and grabbed the bulge in Matt's pants, stroking his rigid cock through the fabric. "Oh yeah, real nice." He smirked and then pulled away. "I hope you don't mind, I mean, I hope you're okay with this."

"Yeah, it felt nice. Could I, maybe, I mean, could I...?"

Scott answered by grabbing Matt's hand and placing it right on his bulge. "Get a good feel, buddy." After Matt had groped him for a moment, he handed Matt the joint. "Might as well improve on this."

Scott unzipped his own fly then reached over and unzipped Matt's, wriggling his fingers through the fly of the boxers to wrap his hand directly around Matt's dick. It wasn't the first time that someone had handled Matt's dick, but he had fantasized about Scott doing it without any hope of it happening.

He handed the joint to Scott who looked at him, stroking Matt. "Please?" Matt realized that he really could and dropped his hand back into Scott's lap, snaking it in to play with what was inside. It was hot and damp and Matt got even harder just from touching it as it swelled in Matt's hand. He had seen Scott's dick a few times, but never hard. Now that he held it in his hand, he knew he wanted to see it.

He was briefly disappointed when Scott pulled his hand away again, but it was only to unbutton his shorts, and push everything down to his ankles. "Hope you don't mind my bare ass on your couch." It was Matt's fondest wish, every time they had sat there playing video games in their boxers. He sat with his thick pink boner poking from a tangle of curly red pubes up against his t-shirt, a tiny wet spot spreading from the head. "Lemme see yours," said Scott, and Matt quickly obliged, kicking his jeans and boxers across the room.

They sat on the couch for a bit, smoking, stroking each other and themselves, and kissing. Matt had trimmed his pubes short after liking the look in a pic he saw on the Internet while jacking off. Scott ran his thumb over the blond stubble "Nice tight pubes, I might have to do that myself." Matt, his fingers tangled in Scott's pubes, thought "don't you dare," but just went in for a kiss.

Scott broke from the kiss, looked into Matt's eyes for a moment, licked his lips, and dropped his face into his friend's lap. Matt almost lost it watching the red curly hair bob up and down in his lap as Scott sucked his dick. He had been blown five, maybe six times before, but the others didn't matter right now.

Scott looked up at him, eyes wide in expectation, then he let Matt's dick slip from his mouth. The head landed on Matt's polo shirt, leaving a damp mark from Scott's spit.

"Um, is it okay if I, I mean, did you like it?"

Matt responded by pulling Scott into a kiss, their tongues thrusting against each other as their dicks did the same between their bellies. Scott's dick left a cool damp trail against the smooth skin of Matt's belly. Suddenly aggressive, he pushed Scott back onto the couch, wrestling with him, as their hands went to new places, grabbing each other's butts as they hugged even closer, then he slid down between Scott's legs to claim his prize.

Scott tugged off his t-shirt, pulling it past solid abs covered with a trail of hair that fanned out to his pink nipples in freckled skin, before leaning back contentedly, his arms behind his head, the joint stuck between his teeth. "This is the life. A blowjob and a toke. I could never get...I mean, this is living the life."

Matt went up and down on Scott's dick, using whatever his limited experience had taught him. He felt Scott tense and braced himself for the eruption into his mouth, but Scott pried his dick away. "Your turn, bro. You gotta try this." He reached down and helped Matt out of his polo, then slid off the couch to kneel on the floor.

Matt looked past the sight of Scott sucking his dick, across Scott's broad back to the bristle of copper hairs between his butt cheeks. Scott was right. This was the life. He cautiously ran a finger down Scott's spine to the treasure in front of him.

As his fingers grazed the hairs, Scott looked up at him and spat out his dick. Matt snatched his hand away, fearful that he had transgressed, but instead of a rebuke, Scott said, "Could we do this on your bed, and um, could you be generous with the pot again?"

Emboldened by the sight of his best friend kneeling between his legs, he spoke a fantasy. "Shouldn't it be ass for grass, dude?"

"Okay, but I want more head first. And the bed. Pretty please." Scott licked at Matt's balls, which tickled a little, but Matt liked it. "And I want to taste you again."

"We got a deal, Matty boy." He stretched out on Matt's bed, his dick pointing skyward. When Matt joined him, he flipped around before Matt could move in for a kiss. "We gotta sixty-nine," diving onto Matt's dick while pointing his own at Matt's mouth. Matt slid his mouth down, his nose approaching Scott's hairy balls, and as he contemplated licking them, he wondered if his friend had always been like this and how he had failed to notice. "Play with my ass, dude. Go on," he heard from between his legs.

Even though he touched his own hole occasionally when jacking off, it felt thrilling and forbidden to touch Scott's, though the thought had fueled his fantasies since high school. As his fingers curled into the damp and furry recesses, he felt his dick leak into Scott's mouth and his balls tightened.

Scott noticed and said, "Don't come yet, bro, remember you're getting my ass today."

Matt felt his dick twitch. He had never been so hard, and his whole body was just an extension of his dick. "I don't know how long I can hold off."

"Then let's do it! Time for ass for grass, go for it." Scott rolled onto his back and raised his legs, hooking his arms around them. They had been friends since kindergarten, but Matt had never seen Scott's asshole, though he had played with his own wondering about his friend's.

A starburst of copper-colored hair surrounded a smooth pink star. Like a star it had some sort of gravitational pull on Matt and he could feel his dick start to drip onto the rumpled sheets.

"You can stick it in me, but go slow. It's been a while."

"You've done this?"

"Two years ago at skateboard camp. Partly to pay for grass and partly because I liked it. Lube me up."

Matt grabbed the hand lotion he used for jacking off. "Will this do?" While his brain chanted a mantra of "please say yes."

"Yeah, slick me and you up good. Use your fingers on me."

His hand trembling a little, he dabbed a finger into Scott's butthole, surprised at the tightness, even though he had done the same to himself. He continued playing with his friend's ass, squirting a little more lotion, until Scott reached down and grabbed Matt's dick, positioning it at his hole.

"Now slick yourself up. Go slow. Have you done this before?"

"Uh, no." It irked Matt a bit that his own sexual experience amounted to a few furtive handjobs and blowjobs, while his so-called straight best friend had already taken it up the ass that Matt had been fantasizing about since junior high, the same time that Scott had began his exploration of girls.

"You're gonna love it, and I wish I had saved it for you." Scott blushed a little at the revelation.

"I think I kinda saved mine for you."

Scott blushed even deeper.

The lotion on his dick felt cold at first. Knowing how tight Scott's hole felt around his finger, Matt wondered how his dick would fit in and his dick skittered across the slick hole a few times before Scott relaxed and the tip slipped in. As he pushed, he felt a tightness, almost a pinch, around the head of his dick. His fears that he might be hurting his friend were dispelled when Scott pushed his ass against him, his dick sliding in with a suddenness that surprised both of them a little, and they gasped simultaneously.

Scott looked over at the remains of the joint as it gave up its last tendril of smoke. "Too bad you don't have another one of those nearby. It'd be rad to smoke while fucking. Next time."

Matt recorded in the back of his mind the expectation of a next time, as his dick slid slowly into his best friend, until his short blond pubes meshed with the reddish hairs between Scott's legs. He let out a brief moan and had to stop himself from shooting his load then and there. No way would his first time fucking, and this of all asses, be over seconds after it had begun.

Matt paused, feeling the tightness and warmth of his friend's hole around his dick. He could feel the pre-cum trickling out of his dick, which felt harder than it had ever been, twitching a little as he just held it there in Scott's ass. Beneath him was Scott's toned body, and he ran his fingers over Scott's abs, something he had wanted to do for years. Scott let out a little giggle, the movement wiggling Matt's dick, the best sensation he had ever had.

They both let out brief cries as Matt eased a couple of inches of dick back out of Scott's ass, then sank back inside, building up to a rhythm, encouraged by Scott's smiles and laughs. Scott's ass felt hot and tight around Matt's dick as he plunged in and out, his breath quickening.

As Scott clutched at his ass to pull him in deeper, Matt found himself thinking that his friend was beautiful, and dipped his head in so they could exchange kisses. As their bodies pressed together, Matt could feel Scott's dick pulsate between them. It too was leaking pre-cum, making a visible trail on Scott's belly.

A few times he thought he would lose it early, but his buzz from the pot helped him prolong the experience. He looked down with some surprise at the sight of his dick pistoning in and out of his best friend's hole. What better friend could there be, right? Though his dick wasn't much larger than Scott's, it looked massive as it slid in and out of his friend's hole, the red hairs clinging to it when he pulled back as if trying to pull him back deep inside.

The tension built in his balls as they worked their bodies against each other, a thin layer of sweat covering them. Matt licked the salty taste of Scott's neck as he continued work the tight hole. He had never felt anything better.

They were wordless for a bit, until Scott said, "fuck, man, I think I'm going to shoot."

Matt shoved his pulsating dick deep into his best friend's ass, yelling, "Oh, fuck, I'm shooting." With a series of grunts, he closed his eyes and pumped his load deep into Scott.

In response, Scott's dick spurted between the two of them, and when Matt opened his eyes, he saw some of Scott's juice sprayed from chest to chin. It struck the two of them as funny and they started laughing. Matt thought he should pull out, but Scott locked his legs around him until Matt's dick softened and slithered out of its own accord. Meanwhile they laughed and licked whatever cum they could reach off each other, pausing to kiss and share the taste of Scott's load.

They lay on the bed together, their bodies shining with a mixture of sweat and cum, when Matt asked the question he'd been thinking about since Scott started blowing him. "So what's with all this? I thought that you were straight, what with all the girls you were boning."

"You can be bi and still bone a lot of girls. And like getting boned by a cute guy." He craned his neck for a kiss, which he got. "What about you?"

"You can be gay and not have the nerve to tell your best friend."

"Maybe next time, you'll let me have your ass."

Matt snorted. "You can fuck my ass when you start paying for the weed you bum off me."

Scott shot up and grabbed his wallet from his shorts, opening it and letting a shower of crumpled bills and drops of cum rain across Matt's chest and stomach. The largest, a twenty, landed directly on the head of his dick. Scott flopped down on top of Matt, giving him a quick peck on the lips. "Here's payment for now and in advance. I can manage that now, I'm a free man."

They both started laughing. Matt thought about how they would laugh again when it came time to spend that money. He placed his hands on his best friend's ass. "Scott, I think we got a deal here."

"Okay, and from now on, I always get to ride shotgun." That was the day that Scott starting calling Matt's dick "shotgun."

Matt just grabbed his stash and with his dick already hardening again rolled another.

"You can ride shotgun whenever you want."

The Pup Who Chased the Lavender Train

Phillip Joy

*T*he words on the computer screen blurred together. I slumped
lower onto the couch. *Oh god! Come on, Ben, you only have
thirty more papers left to mark.* The thought dragged me down
even further than the pillows. *If I have to type "Not in APA for-
mat" one more time I think I will lose it. I spent twenty minutes in
class going over this.* The life of a TA was not the glamourous one
I thought it would be when I signed up for grad school. And no,
I never honestly thought it would be stellar but I didn't think the
kids would be so careless.

My roommate Jeff stepped out of his bedroom with yet a different jacket. "Is this better?"

It looked the same to me. "Definitely."

He pouted. "I think it's too stuffy."

"Aren't you going to be surrounded by hipsters tonight?"

"Damn right. Nothing draws the long beards like a late-night
tattoo art show." He tugged at his sleeves. "Ain't no way I won't
get some ass."

I groaned at his grammar. Jeff and I disagreed about many
things—thankfully not the rent. He likened his men to cigarettes:
skinny, stinky, and easily thrown to the curb.

I reached for my coffee, only to find grinds floating in the last few cold mouthfuls. I downed it anyway and brought up the next paper. The title read "An Introduction to the Female Reproduction System." I groaned and immediately closed the file. "Don't wait up," Jeff yelled as he left. "Unless you want to watch."

I shoved the laptop away and got up to stretch.

How am I ever going to get all these done before Prof. Connor wants the marks entered? Impossible without medication. And the coffee's not doing it.

When my roommate felt stressed he did a little toke.

I weaved my way around the stacks of health textbooks, art histories, dirty clothes, and unfinished paper mache figures that littered the apartment. I crept into Jeff's room and went immediately to his dresser where I knew he kept his stash. I opened the top drawer, but found nothing but socks and underwear, which wear threadbare tighty whities. I placed them back and moved onto the next drawer. An array of pop culture references plastered on T-shirts filled me eyes. I wasted no time rooting through his shirts and quickly opened the last drawer. My eyes fell upon row after row of neatly ordered clear sandwich bags, each carefully labeled, each filled with clumps of greenish-brown buds.

Good lord, I knew he liked his weed but I had no idea he liked it this much. They're even fucking alphabetized. If only he was this organized with his art shit.

I pulled out my phone and googled "how to roll a joint" and was soon on a video offering a step-by-step guide. I found all the supplies I needed, including Jeff's grinder, his stack of papers, and some cardboard neatly folded like an accordion tucked away in the corner. I arranged four white pieces across the top of the dresser. *Might as well make a few just in case one doesn't really do anything.* One in particular caught my eye: "Lavender Trainwreck" had a slight purple hue with orange hairs. *Maybe it will even taste like lavender.* I opened the bag and took a whiff; I had to suppress a gag at its pungent aroma; definitely not a fragrant sachet.

I threw some into the grinder. I then transformed the leaf buds into what the website called "shake" and arranged a line of it onto each of the papers. Rolling them, however, turned out to be more challenging than I expected. I eventually got them to resemble something like very fat misshapen cigarettes.

Back on the coach, I made myself comfortable and lit the first one. Placing my mouth on the home-made filter, I inhaled. A sharp burn raced down my throat and settled into my chest. I held it until I exploded, smoke and coughs ripping me open. I drew another and then another until only a small hot bit remained of the joint, which I dropped into the empty soda can next to me. Determined to start grading again, I took up my laptop once more. As I began to read, the words moved ahead of me. I raced to catch them but before I could they started to dance, merging and embracing each other. The curves of the "S" wrapping and pulling the "T" into itself, transforming and re-arranging, telling tell me their secrets, expanding me. The student who wrote this was beyond brilliant. I was on the precipice of new understanding when the screen started to blink and then went black. *What the fuck?* I must have been reading the same paper again and again...and not realize the laptop's battery had given up the ghost. I felt less frustrated and hungrier.

I pushed the dead computer away, plugging it into the wall outlet. I made my way to the fridge and found it humming along but empty except for mustard, some ketchup, and a few bottles of soda. The cupboards were in slightly better shape, stocked with cans of soup, green beans, and bag of half-used rice. *Nothing useful here. What I need is some good breakfast shit—cereal, peanut butter, or eggs. Damn, I need to go to the store.*

It should have been cold outside but my body didn't feel it. The snow, falling from the clear black skies, reminded me of sliver glitter floating down from a disco. *I wonder if that's what heaven is like.* I noticed that there were no sounds, not even the crunch of the snow under my boots, it was as if the whole world decided to stop everything and admire its own beauty. I felt like I was the only person alive, walking to the lone corner market still open at that hour.

The glare of fluorescent lights overhead stung my eyes; and their buzzing hurt my ears. I didn't recall picking up a basket, but when I started reaching for package after package of colorful, gummy animals, I had the basket at hand. I wondered around until I found the peanut butter and added it to my growing order. The cereal aisle was my next stop.

"Cereal is the best when you are high, especially the sugary kind."

"Yeah?"

Behind me stood a cute boy. Chestnut brown hair waved down to his shoulders, big brown eyes that echoed his smile.

"Kinda obvious you have the munchies." He stepped closer, looking at my haul and chuckled. "Here," he said, and, with an arm around my shoulder, guided me down the aisle. "These are my favorite." The tiger on the box agreed. "They're grrreat"

"I couldn't eat the whole box myself. You'd have to have some too." *Did I just invite this guy to my place?* It was as if my brain had its filter turned off and words were just slipping out.

He reached at my waist, and I thought he was going to grab my crotch right there in the market, but instead he pulled out one of the remaining joints, which I must have shoved in my pocket and utterly forgotten. "And we could start by sharing these."

His name was Mitchell and we stood huddled in the back alley of the store. As he held his lighter up to me, my body began pulsating from his closeness. He lit the joint hanging from my mouth and I managed to inhale without coughing. I felt the weed seep through my extremities, seeping away my nerves and bringing a sense of euphoria. *Maybe it's the boy making me feel this giddy and not the weed.*

Mitchell brushed my hand when he took the joint. I stared as he took his first drag. The way his mouth opened slightly, the way his lips wrapped around the filter, and the slight rise of his shoulders as he inhaled. He was perfection made real. *Yep, it's definitely the boy making me high.*

The snow fell in bigger flakes and Mitchell reached into his knapsack, pulling out a hat. Adjusting it over his mop of hair, he winked at me "So what do you think? Is it me?"

The hat, white-furred with tips of gray at the pointy ears, transformed him into a wolf cub.

"That is awesome." I took two steps closer to him and reached up to run my fingers over it. My hands lingered on the soft fur; I began petting him like a puppy. A lop-sided grin had spread across his face. I couldn't stop from kissing him. Time stopped and there was nothing but the velvet of those lips and light touches of the snowflakes across my exposed skin. His tongue entered my mouth. Our fingers found each other's and the warmth of his body flowed into me. When we finally parted, echoes of laughter followed us as we ran down the alley towards my place.

*H*e passed me the third joint, already half gone. The haze of our smoked swirled around the room leaving it smelling like burnt popcorn infused with floral undertones. He was sitting cross-legged on the floor eating directly from the cereal box, spilling crumbs all over the beige carpet. I slipped my hand into the box with his, giving him a kiss in the process.

"Any toy surprise?"

"Maybe...but not in the box." Mitchell pushed me backed and kissed me.

"You're such an eager little wolf."

He gave a short howl as he pounced onto my chest, trying to take off my shirt.. "I'm your wolf puppy." He began to lick my neck, slobbering all over me, and I found my dick harder than its ever been, constrained in my tight jeans.

He proceeded to nibble at my ears.. I tried to change positions. But his body was heavy and, like an unruly puppy, he wasn't budging. He began nudging his head into me, whimpering, needing my full attention. His soft hair tickling me each time he nuzzled into me. Panting, he sat on my chest looked at me with his big brown eyes. I reached up and patted his head, stroked behind his ear. He barked in his pleasure. I wrestled him off me and onto his back. With our positions reversed, I slid my hands up under his shirt to rub his belly, feel the thick fur on it and on his chest. His foot started shaking and I laughed at his silliness.

"Who's a good boy? Are you a good boy?" I said.

Again, he barked and my hand slowly moved lower, following the trail to his crotch. My fingers traced the outline of his bulge, feeling it twitch. I worked the button of his jeans opened and pulled out his erect uncut cock. When I pulled back his foreskin his head glistened with more pre-cum than I had ever seen before. My thumb gently traced around his head, collecting the clear fluid on it. I gave him my thumb and watched him as he licked it clean. I never imagined what a turn-on it would be. I bent down to kiss him, hoping to taste the saltiness in his mouth. A deep ache grew within me. I wanted to hear and see him whimper and beg for sex. I got up, took off all my clothes, and sat on the couch.

"Come here, pup."

He stripped. I admired the dark hair on his body. On all fours he crawled to me and placed his head in my lap, within an inch of my hard dick, and whimpered in anticipation.

"Go ahead."

That was all the invitation he needed. He took my hard cock into his mouth. Slowly licking the full length of my shaft before running his tongue over my head. I grabbed his hair and pushed him down deeper, forcing him to take it all. I loved hearing him whimper as he sucked me. Just when I thought he would deep throat me, I pinched his ear. I didn't want the night to end so soon. I wanted to plow that furry ass.

He looked up at me with wide eyes.

"Beg me to fuck you, pup."

He yipped and began crawling fast in circles as if chasing his tail.

I moved behind him and gently ran my hands over his back, tracing the curve of his spine all the way down to his ass, sheer perfection, rounded, matted with sweaty hair. I pressing my fingers into his flesh, I pushed his ass cheeks apart until he was fully exposed to me. I wanted to tease him, to make him squirm before I filled him with my hard cock. I bent close and blew softly. His body quivered. I pressed my lips to his eager hole, kissing it. He moaned as he pressed back into me. I started to work my tongue into his hole, exploring it. Eating his ass was a new high for me, sweet-tasting and addictive. I could not get my tongue deep enough. His body moved in response to my probing, edging me on. I leaned back again to admire him. A primal growl vibrated through his body and I knew he was demanding more attention.

I spat into his greedy little hole. For a split second, I watched as my spit run down it before working it into him with my finger. He howled as if he truly was a wolf baying at the moon. My fingers disappeared deeper inside him. And the next howl quickly turned into little pup grunts as I finger fucked him.

He let out a little whimper when I withdrew. He looked back at me, eagerness twinkling in his eyes, and whimpered again. Playfully, he started wiggling his ass. I could almost picture a furry tail wagging back and forth. I slapped his behind; hard to settle him down and inched closer to him, digging my fingers into his hips. Our bodies connected. My cock grinding into his behind. I teased him, running my cock over his hole. Slowly, I pushed my head into him. I went deeper into him, his body twitching until I was completely inside him. I ran my hands up his back as I began to fuck him. His body responding to my thrusts. We lost ourselves in blind ecstasy, fucking like wild dogs. I lost all sense of myself as a cloud of pure pleasure enveloped the essence of my being. I couldn't hold back much longer. He squeezed his glutes together, tightening his grip on my cock. I exploded inside him. Everything but his body was burned out of my existence in a white-hot blaze of stars. Breathless, I fell onto his sweaty back.

We lay like this for eternity until my senses began to come back. I started licking his neck, tasting his saltiness. My hand soon found his cock and I started jerking him off. His cock head was so wet that may hand easily glided up and down the length of his shaft. I played with his foreskin, sliding it back and forth over his head. His puppy pants intensified as his muscles tightened and his feet flexed. He was ready to come and I wanted to see it. I leaned over him just in time to see his cum shoot forth, erupting in a geyser of milky spunk that covered in chest, his crotch, and my hand. I wanted every last drop of his cum so I pushed his fore-skin over his head on last time. It flowed into my hand. He rolled over and we locked eyes. I lifted my dripping fingers to his face once again. He broke into his lop-sided grin and took my fingers into his mouth. Like a good puppy he licked them clean. Next, his tongue was all over my face in big, puppy licks.

"Silly boy" I whispered as I tousled his hair more.

He gave one more whimper before nestling into my chest and closing his eyes.

The sound of the deadbolt on the front door woke me. I slipped out from beneath Mitchell as Jeff walked into the apartment.

"Seems like you had more fun than me tonight," he said as he grabbed a soda from the fridge. "I can smell you smoked my weed. Glad someone lit up. The art show was a bust. I don't mind a bunch of no talent pretentious hacks showing off, but they were straight edge."

He swallowed a third of the soda, his adam's apple bobbing. He let out a belch. "He's looks...familiar."

"Oh?" I scratched the boy's back, making him arch and stretch. He yawned and smacked his lips and murmured. He blinked at us.

"Holy shit, that's my dealer's kid!"

A Friendly Ghostbusting

Charles Payseur

*F*irst, a voice. "Boxfield Psychiatric Prison, lovingly called the Box by those in the know, stands in mockery of the modern age."

Then video, digitized obviously, but using something like a Super 8, the film quality terrible and bringing to mind home movies from hell. The film shows a wide lawn, green and neat, and waiting in supplication of the enormous building rising up above it. A lone road arcs toward a columned entryway.

"From 1879 to 1979 it saw more than ten thousand...well, they called them patients, passed through its doors, committed against their wills for crimes deemed too terrible to be born of a sane mind."

Image montage of faces, mugshots. Fairly fast, no one image lingering too long, because it's not like the place was a who's who of crime. This wasn't maximum security, after all, and all the research states that most of the people committed to the Box were, at best, regionally notorious.

"What makes the Box special, though, is not how many men, women, and children passed through its doors, but rather how many passed on while inside. Records indicate that nearly two-thirds would never be released save for to the tender embrace of the waiting earth. Perhaps a mercy, if the rumors of what went on after hours are to be believed."

Cas sighed and hit pause, wondering if it was a strong enough opening to what was sure to be his most popular series yet. Was it too history heavy? Or too macabre? He was a ghost hunter, yes, but people would be turned off his FaceTube channel if he didn't bring enough of his trademark charm and humor to the proceedings. He took another bite of brownie and hoped it would just fucking relax him already. What was Caspar the Friendly Ghostbuster, after all, without that tongue-in-cheek wit his fans knew and loved? He sighed again and slipped the headphones from his ears. All work and no play made Cas a dull internet celebrity, and he looked out the window of the van to see that the same columned entrance he had seen in the video was just coming into view.

"Hey," he said, reaching over to shove Rina, his driver, tech support, and oldest friend, in the shoulder, "why didn't you tell me we were there already?"

"I did," Rina said, rolling her eyes. She had been with him since the first haunted house, both of them still in college and Cas desperate to impress a guy who claimed anyone who stayed the night in the old Graham place would have to be incredibly brave. What had his name been? Tad? Erik? He shook his head and realized that Rina was still talking.

"Sorry, what?" he asked, and Rina sucked in a breath and said something in Spanish he didn't understand, then slowed the car to a stop a good two hundred yards from the main stairs.

"I said, I've been trying to get your attention for the past ten minutes," she said, gesturing to his laptop and the tray half-full of pot brownies, "but as usual you've been too swept up in *the magic* to bother listening."

"You don't have to be—" Cas said, but Rina just talked over him.

"I've been *trying* to ask you if you have that paper you got the owners to sign. The waiver. You know, so we don't get kicked out and arrested for being here."

Cas reached into his pocket and produced the paper in question. "Signed and sealed," he said, smiling. The world was wearing a pleasant fog, but even through it he could feel his heart beating fast, the fear threatening to overtake his calm. "They were glad to get the press. Apparently they're selling to a theme park that's going to turn it into Halloween Town or something like that and the publicity will help ahead of the demolition and reconstruction."

Rina clucked her tongue and looked back at the enormous building. "Seems almost a shame," she said. "Lots of history there."

The sound of an engine interrupted whatever else she was going to say, and they both turned to see a motorbike speed down the lane behind and then around them, kicking up a wake of dust as it zipped to the Box. The figure on the bike was a blur. The only thing Cas could make out was the large lettering on the back of the leather jacket the rider wore that read: The Yokai Slayer. Cas growled.

"Speaking of history," Rina said, but Cas was already out of the car and rushing after the bike, which stopped about halfway between them and the building.

"Hey," Cas shouted. "Hey! What do you think you're doing here?" He wasn't sure if his voice was loud enough to be heard over the roar of the engine, which the rider kept obnoxiously revving. "Hey!"

Finally, when Cas was ten feet away, the engine cut off and the rider flipped down the kickstand, stood, and peeled off the sleek riding helmet that encased their head. Cas swallowed as the black hair, shoulder length and straight as a blade, cascaded down from its imprisonment, and then the man turned and it was all Cas could do not to gape at him standing there, six feet of lean muscle that looked damn fine in leather. Soft brown eyes regarded him, and Cas remembered his anger, his frown returning doubly as he stomped forward.

"What the hell do you think you're doing here, Yasahiro?" Cas asked, flinching at the smile that spread on the other man's face.

"No one calls me that," he said, dismounting the bike and setting his helmet on the seat. Then, with a flourish, he drew something forth from his jacket, something he must have been carrying in there the entire trip. Cas was unsurprised when he recognized the cover of this month's *People*. Annoyed, yes, but not surprised. Cas felt his hands clench as he read the caption of the picture Yasahiro was pointing at, his own striking profile next to the teaser "Someone call a Hiro?"

"You're still the punk who nearly left the Careyville graveyard crying," Cas said. It wasn't fair. Didn't he get just as much traffic as Yasahiro? Didn't he have just as clever a gimmick? Why wasn't it his face in the bottom left beneath Julia Roberts in a bikini?

"That was a long time ago," Yasahiro said, and stuck out his tongue in rebuttal.

"Real mature," Cas said.

"Hey, maturity is for old men, gramps," Yasa said, because Cas wouldn't even think of him with that stupid name.

"I'm only two years older than you are," Cas said, hands clenching tighter and he realized too late that he was mangling his written permission to be here. He smiled, remembering. "Anyway, you need to be going. I'm getting ready to begin my work and don't want to have to call the cops to clear out trespassers."

Yasa shook his head and replaced the magazine into his jacket, pulled out in its place a folded piece of paper, and Cas felt his body tense. It couldn't be…

"I'm not trespassing," Yasa said, unfolding the paper and holding it forward. It looked exactly like Cas'. "Perhaps you should have stipulated in your agreement that you'd have sole rights to use the property. Because the developers seemed to think that extra publicity was extra good."

Why'd it have to be Yasa? Cas cursed under his breath and turned sharply, stomped back to the car where Rina was waiting, looking like it was all she could do to suppress her laughter.

"We're leaving," Cas said, his calm completely gone. Like hell he'd share with Yasa. Not when the little sneak had made him look like a fool, not when Cas had taught him the ins and outs of ghost hunting only to be abandoned and embarrassed.

"Caspar..." Rina said, and Cas cursed out loud this time, not bothering to hide his anger. The way she said his name told him all he needed to know. That they couldn't walk away now. Not with all the promoting they'd done about it. Not with the whispers that he was losing his step, that Hiro the Yokai Slayer was younger, hotter, and more exciting. Which completely ignored the fact that Yasa barely bothered to edit his content, that he didn't construct a narrative around his investigations. That he shot it all with a little handheld that shook and blurred at key moments. Cas kicked the car, felt pain shoot through his foot, cursed again. Why'd it have to be Yasa?

"Fine," Cas said, opening the door and slipping inside, drawing his laptop back up and picking up his headphones from where they had fallen. "Fine. We'll stay. But I'm not working with him. He can go off and do whatever and we'll start after I get the opener finished." And he shut the car door before Rina could respond.

Cas posted his opener and his preliminary comments on the game plan. EMS, question and answer, the typical kind of thing. The Box was supposed to be haunted, but very little was known as to just how. It really had been under lock and key even after closing, until recently when the land had become worth something and sold off. There were rumors of the experiments done on patients, though, horrible things that glutted the grave-yard like Cas at an all-you-can-eat buffet during a particularly strong case of the munchies.

Rina had all the audio set up, had mapped out the area she wanted him to investigate. She was his eyes and ears from the car, able to guide him and monitor activity across all their tech. Cas' job was to go inside, to face the actual ghosts and dangers the night would bring.

"Okay, standard procedure," she said as she hooked up the cameras on his vest and helmet, one looking outward, one pointed at his face, both with night vision fittings to make them feel authentic, though they didn't really help Cas any.

"Just tell me he said that he'd keep his distance," Cas said, knowing that somehow, despite how Yasa had betrayed them both, Rina didn't hold a grudge. He had seen them talking as he had sulked in the car and worked on his videos and polished off more the brownies. The world was starting to take on a pleasant cast but nothing would cut through his apprehension fully.

"You know he feels bad about how it went at the brewery," Rina said. Cas shot her a look and she sighed. "He said that he'd try to stay out of your way."

"Good," Cas said, and made his way to the front steps of the Box, going over his route in his mind, taking a breath before beginning his ascent.

His mind was hazy, and he knew he shouldn't have taken more of the brownies—delayed release, possibility of overdose, blah blah. He tried to keep his mind on business, but the pot and the nerves about working so close to Yasa had his stomach roiling. He'd add narration afterward, not trusting his voice right then. Not like he'd remember a script even if he had written one.

The front hall was old but not in terrible condition, and led a short distance before emptying out into the reception area.

"Almost like it's just closed for the weekend, right?" a voice asked from behind him and Cas couldn't help but giving a small shriek, immediately regretting it as he recognized Yasa's laugh, which should have been annoying but was just infuriating for how it made Cas' heart beat a bit faster, the darkness luckily hiding the flush in his cheeks.

"Damn it, Yasa!" Cas said, turning to face his former friend and pupil. And almost more, though they had never—Cas growled at the thought, willing it away.

"You know you're still cute when you're mad," Yasa said, and Cas turned and started walking into the darkness of the reception area, heard Yasa hurry to follow close behind him.

"Shouldn't you be off making your own video and not getting in the middle of mine?" Cas asked.

"You used to like me in your videos," Yasa said, and Cas fought the urge to scream. Did the man have some gift to know exactly what would hurt the most? What would twist the knife in his back a little deeper?

"Before you sold me out," Cas said, not caring where he went now, pushing his way through a door into a long corridor. He wasn't paying attention to the map anymore, just wanted to be moving, preferably away from Yasa. "Before you took video of me without my permission to make me look like an idiot."

Yasa snorted, and Cas gritted his teeth and turned, pushed through another door, found himself in what might have been a cafeteria, another large room with chairs and an area that might have been a kitchen.

"You were always saying that I had to do my own thing, find my own angle," Yasa said. "Are you really angry that I finally took your advice, or that I ended up doing better than you thought I would?"

Cas moved across the cafeteria into another room, maybe a group therapy room or a recreation area. It was mostly empty, and he was afraid of running out of places to go.

"You made it look like I didn't believe," Cas said, remembering the viral video, the accusations, the loss of followers and offers to investigate. All because Yasa had filmed him having a fake question and answer pretending, *pretending* to be making up his findings. It was a joke, just blowing off steam, dealing with a stupid thing someone had posted about him online. He had just had a bad breakup and he was feeling angry, bitter. He said things he shouldn't have... Why was he trying to justify himself? He was the one betrayed.

"I'm sorry," Yasa said as Cas walked through another door, and his voice was different now, less confrontational, less sarcastic. "I...I screwed it all up. I was afraid."

"Afraid of what?" Cas asked. It wasn't like he had ever been mean or insulting to Yasa. He had always tried to be friendly, perhaps too much so because he had been attracted to Yasa from the start, from their first meeting, and yet because he was with someone at the time couldn't act on it.

"Afraid that you'd find someone else," Yasa blurted out, and Cas paused as he walked through another door.

"What do you mean?" he asked. "I had just broken up—"

"With Brad, I know," Yasa said. It all came rushing back like a bad soap opera. Brad. They'd never been all that serious, but after Cas met Yasa, Brad had gotten clingy, jealous. Was that what kept him around so long, that he didn't want to be dumped for someone else? That he could see that Cas would rather be with Yasa and was determined to repay Cas for the hurt it must have caused.

"And I was so happy about that," Yasa went on. "Happy that he'd be gone and maybe, maybe...but you always saw me as your sidekick, as your buddy. I didn't think you could... I didn't think that I could stand if you started seeing someone new. I was sure you would. I mean, look at you. And I...I've never had a relationship last more than a week."

Wait, was he saying what Cas thought he was saying? That he...that he wanted to be with him all along? Not as friends, but as lovers? And something inside Cas broke at that. Was he really so weak, to feel such elation at hearing those words? It felt like he was betraying himself this time, because he had hoped to hear Yasa say that for so long. He had always...always hoped that there was something else; some way that Yasa hadn't meant to hurt him. Yasa was part of the reason for his breakup, after all, Brad accusing Cas of spending too much time with him, being too close to him. And Cas had thought that, maybe, with him out of the way, that maybe he could have... He swung around to face Yasa.

"Why didn't you just say something?" Cas demanded, as much of himself and of Yasa, because his silence had been just as damning.

"I'm sorry," Yasa said again.

"Sorry for what?" Cas asked, hands balled into tight fists. "Sorry for making me look like a fake? For setting me back a year? A year of begging and apologizing and working my ass off to make up for five stupid fucking minutes that were supposed to be for you and me and not..." Cas broke off, not trusting himself to say anything more.

No one spoke, and Cas let his eyes rest on Yasa's face. His eyes were black circles in the darkness, his face covered in shadows but Cas could see the sadness there, the hesitation, the hurt. Why didn't it feel better? He had imagined laying into Yasa ever since they had parted ways, and yet now that the man himself was standing in front of him, tight body mere inches away, why did he want nothing more than to wrap his arms around those tired-looking shoulders and forgive? What was he thinking?

"Caspar..." Yasa said, and Cas wanted to curse. The way Yasa said his name told him all he needed to know.

"Caspar..." came his name again, but Yasa hadn't spoken. Neither had Cas. The air in the room seemed to vibrate, seemed to come alive with static. Every hair on Cas' body stood up, and his breathing paused as he swallowed and tried to place where the voice had come from.

"Caspar..." it came again. Definitely behind him and definitely not a hallucination caused by the pot. He swore inwardly, at the same time hoping that his equipment was picking it up. Where were they? Were they still in the area that Rina had mapped out? Cas realized he didn't know. He looked up into Yasa's face, which was fixed on the space behind him. It looked like he was watching something. Cas gritted his teeth and turned.

What did a voice even look like? He'd seen orbs before. Once or twice a face in a reflection. Once he had even captured the sound of a child laughing, though at the time he hadn't heard anything. Only listening to the audio on playback with filters applied did it sound like anything. But this...

When movies showed ghosts they were bright, glowing and translucent, specters that floated and flitted. Even in his videos people got more excited about small bits of dust than they did anything else. But this... Could darkness somehow be even darker? Because it wasn't a light that greeted him. Not a warm glow. It was a shadow on darkness, the knowledge that something was moving there, the knowledge that something capable of speech had just addressed him personally and yet he could only see it by the slithering movement of the darkness that couldn't be explained by passing cars or doors swinging shut.

"Caspar..." the voice said a third time, and Cas swallowed, knowing that the video was still rolling, that despite everything this was a chance at something—something amazing. He swallowed again, cleared his throat, felt Yasa's hand on his shoulder squeezing a warning, but Cas wasn't about to be scared off by a ghost, no matter how unique it was.

"I'm here," Cas said, and before he could think he felt the room drop ten degrees and gasped involuntarily. The darkness in front of him swirled, growing darker and darker, and he wasn't sure what he was looking at, wasn't sure of much except that he couldn't move. Did it make him a terrible person that he was glad that Yasa was there? He still refused to forgive him, but his presence there was familiar and reassuring and an anchor in this—

The darkness swelled forward and Cas' eyes widened. He willed his body to move but it refused, remained rooted. Until Cas felt himself shoved to the side hard by the arm on his shoulder, and he fell as Yasa rushed forward with a shout.

"Cas, run!" Yasa said as he leaped at the presence. Then his voice was muffled and his body went rigid and Cas could only watch as the darkness wrapped around him, enveloped him.

"Yasa!" Cas shouted, still unable to move. Why couldn't he move? Why did his body seem bolted to the floor?

There was no response except a vibration in the air, and the temperature continued to plummet. Cas could see his breath as he watched Yasa struggle with something unseen, some force that was holding him and seemed to be buffeting him with spectral energies. Someone had to do something. Where was Rina? Where were the cops? Why couldn't Cas move?

"Caspar..." a voice said, and this time it was Yasa's voice, from Yasa's mouth, but Cas could hear none of the man he had once wished to love in those words. It was cold. It was ice. A shiver shook Cas into motion, and he felt tears well in his eyes. Why wasn't he doing something? He...

"Yasa, I'm sorry," he said, and pushed himself to his feet, took one look at the door and then launched himself at his former protégé. He expected to collide with Yasa's body, to tear him free of whatever was holding him, but he found himself impacted against that force instead.

Immediately Cas felt his blood run cold, colder than walking outside in the heart of a Wisconsin winter. It was like he could feel the hate of the thing in front of him, the malice and violence, and in that moment Cas felt its mind, its truth. How many patients had it tortured? How many souls had it cursed to wander, afraid and crying, after the excruciating deaths he put them through? A doctor should be a healer, not a monster. Cas felt a tightness in his chest, a pain in his eyes. Finally he could see what he was facing, a twisted mockery of humanity stripped down to its core of hate and pain and clutching need for victims.

Yasa cried out, and Cas could feel the pain as his own, could feel the spirit surrounding them revel in it. No. No, he wasn't about to let this happen. He wasn't losing Yasahiro right as they had started talking again, when they might finally get past the false starts and betrayals.

"No," Cas heard himself say, and it was his voice that spoke. His. He pushed forward, found his arms moving against the resistance of the entity, the ghost. It seemed to sense his strength, and he felt pressure tighten around him, heard Yasa whimper as it must have been constricting him as well, but Cas looked into Yasa's eyes and saw a flicker of recognition there, a spark of resistance.

Cas kept reaching, hands finally reaching Yasahiro's side. The contact was electric, and Cas felt the presence around them weaken. *What, can't handle the warmth, asshole?* Cas felt a heat within him, a need, strong and real and his hands found either side of Yasahiro's face, their lips meeting like a clap of thunder and the ice was gone, replaced by something else, by need and raw heat. Whether it was the danger or the pot still lowering his inhibitions, but he didn't care that the ghost was basically watching. In fact, it made it hotter.

"Cas," Yasa said, gasping as they broke the kiss, but Cas wasn't about to stop now, not when he had finally taken the step he had never be willing to try. How many nights had he stared at the ceiling, afraid of the feelings he had for Yasahiro, afraid that he would ruin everything if he tried... He was done waiting.

"I'm sorry," Cas said, and Yasa looked at him as if he was speaking a different language.

"What?" Yasahiro asked. "Why are you—"

Cas kissed him again, hard, hands grasping the back of Yasahiro's neck, not letting him go until the presence lessened even more.

"Sorry that I didn't tell you sooner," Cas said. "That...that I want to be with you."

Yasahiro stared, mouth still open, eyes wide. And then a smile, beautiful, radiant, spread on his face.

"I'm sorry," Yasahiro said. "For...for everything. I would understand if you never wanted to talk to me again."

Cas shook his head. Was there even a ghost at all at this point? Had there ever been? He could feel some sort of lingering cloud of darkness but more and more all he was aware of was Yasa's face in the dim light, the lingering trace of Yasa's lips on his own. Cas jumped forward, and together the two of them tumbled to the floor, a mess of limbs, intentions uniting as they fell, landed, lips somehow finding each other in the press of their bodies.

"Wait," Yasahiro said between kisses, even as Cas' hands moved over his body, reveling in the way it was exactly as hard and yielding as he had always imagined. "We shouldn't...the cameras..."

Cas hadn't even thought of it, but he realized that he was still wearing two cameras, the one on his helmet having been knocked askew somewhere in the excitement. Cas growled, pulled the helmet off and tossed it deeper in the room, did the same with his vest, pulling it off with his shirt and throwing it off into the darkness. The cold was gone entirely, replaced by a raging heat.

"If you don't want to..." Cas said, not wanting to force things if Yasahiro didn't actually want to but really, really hoping he did.

Cas was rewarded by Yasahiro's body rushing back to meet his own, and Cas felt warm hands sweep the naked flesh of his upper body, heard himself moan as fingertips brushed his nipples. He was hard, his whole body burning with need, with anticipation.

Yasahiro paused, and Cas growled, looked down to see that Yasa was pulling at his own shirt. Cas smiled, took advantage of Yasahiro's busy hands to find his fly and quickly undo it. Yasahiro managed only a small yelp as Cas shifted down, pulling Yasa's pants down with a tug and revealing the erection Cas had always fantasized about, long and proud and curving like the blade of that ridiculous katana Yasa held in some of his press photos. Without a second thought, Cas' tongue slipped from between his lips and he ran it up the underside of Yasa's cock from base to head, and was rewarded by a mighty throb and a ragged groan as Yasahiro grew very still. Encouraged, Cas licked again and again, tongue drawing small circles around Yasahiro's head before popping the whole thing into his mouth.

"Casp…" Yasahiro said, and Cas was glad whatever he had been about to say was cut off in a sound of contented pleasure as he sucked down Yasa's length, tongue sliding against tender skin, hand busy massaging Yasa's sack as he worked up and down Yasa's cock. Why had he been angry again? Cas couldn't remember as he moved, mouth slurping slightly as he felt Yasa thrust up with his hips each time Cas descended. Then Cas let it pop out of his mouth and giggled as he felt a bead of drool dribble down his chin. Or was Yasa leaking already? He giggled again and stood, kicked off his shoes. Yasa's eyes widened and he rushed to get his own clothes off, tearing free his shirt and shimmying out of his pants and shoes while Cas watched, wicked smile on his lips.

Yasa began to sit up, perhaps hoping to pay Cas back for before with his mouth, but Cas had other ideas, dropping so that he straddled Yasahiro's waist and met him with his lips instead, pushing him back down with a deep kiss, their tongues dueling from mouth to mouth. Cas pressed a hand to Yashiro's chest, pushed him back to the floor, took his other hand and stuck two fingers in his own mouth, making a show of sucking on them lightly. Yasa pushed against the hand restraining him, but not hard enough to dislodge Cas from his seat. Cas pulled his fingers free and smiled.

"Impatient, are we?" Cas asked, and slowly trailed the hand on Yasa's chest down over a tight stomach, the light hair below Yasa's navel, lower still to the hard cock that was pressed against Cas' own. With his other, newly lubricated fingers, Cas reached back and began touching his own ass, sliding the fingers up so they touched his hole, made small motions inward, his spit easing their way, loosening him up. One hand toying with his own butt and one wrapping around both their cocks at the same time, Cas leaned forward and crushed his lips against Yasa's. He felt a moan work its way out of his throat as his fingers pushed inside him.

Yasa seemed oblivious, distracted by Cas' other hand that had started stroking them together, the heat of their cocks feeding each other, each pushing the other harder and hotter and closer to release. Cas worked his hands at the same time, teasing them both higher, higher, until he could feel himself getting close, a tightness spreading from his stomach outward. He paused, breathing heavy, and disengaged from vigorous kissing, which Yasa protested to with a soft whimper, a begging entreaty not to stop. But Cas had other ideas, emboldened by the drug still coursing through him and the ghost he could still feel trying to regain its control.

Sliding himself down Yasahiro's body, Cas found himself once again face to cock with Yasahiro and wasted no time taking the hard length into his mouth, not caring to be neat, knowing that he would have preferred lube but that this was going to have to do. He'd regret it in the morning, but right then the pot and the adrenaline were telling him he'd regret not doing this much more.

Yasa thought him old, did he? Let him try to keep up. Cas let Yasa's erection pop free from his mouth again and this time Yasa gave a growl of his own, seemed ready to take matters into his own hands but Cas wasn't about to let that happen.

Quickly, Cas shifted, pulled the fingers that had been working him loose free, and standing with feet on either of Yasahiro's waist. With practiced grace, Cas crouched and leaned back, one hand supporting him on the ground between Yasa's knees while the other grabbed Yasa's erection, aimed it as he lowered himself further.

Too late, Yasahiro seemed to realize what Cas was planning and he gave a half-hearted attempt to protest, probably to say it wasn't necessary, that they could do other things, but Cas only wanted one thing at the moment, and that was Yasa inside him. A moment later and he got his wish, pain lacing through his butt as he was less gentle than he could have been. He froze, sucked in a heaving breath and waited a moment, his body relaxing, getting used to Yasa. Then, carefully, he lowered himself more, let go with the hand that was no longer needed and supported himself on both hands splayed behind him. He sank, hissing as Yasa slide deeper and deeper inside him, and felt his own cock twitch into the open air as he reached Yasa's base.

"Caspar..." Yasa said, and Cas smiled, the pain faded. The way Yasa said his name told him all he needed to know. He lifted up an inch, two, slid back down, and Yasa gasped, swore, and then grabbed hold of Cas' ass and started thrusting. Cas felt his whole body shiver as they began to move together, thrust and counter, bodies alive with heat, with sweat, and Cas was surprised it didn't hurt more but any discomfort was already being devoured by the need inside him, the pleasure.

They moved, one of Yasahiro's hands moving from Cas' butt to his bouncing cock, capturing it and stroking it in time to their reckless ascent and descent, and it didn't take long after that. Cas felt like the whole world was exploding, burning, he heard Yasa grunting beneath him, obviously close, obviously needing this just as much as Cas did as he bounced, as he reveled in the feel of Yasahiro's hand bringing him closer, closer.

His eyes shot open as he came, as he heard Yasahiro come into him, their twin moans rising in the darkened room. Only, as pleasure racked Cas' body he saw that the room wasn't dark at all. It was like day. Wasn't it dark? He couldn't seem to remember over the pleasure, over the magic Yasa was performing on his cock and in his ass, but then he saw them. Standing around them. Faces, bodies, ethereal and glowing just like in the movies. And all of them smiling. Suddenly he felt a rush of thoughts, feelings, thousands of voices all speaking at once, thanking him, thanking Yasahiro. They had been trapped, captured, and contained by the hate of the doctor's cruelty, but that was over. They were freed, freed by the passion, the love and forgiveness of Cas and Yasahiro's union, and they were all saying thank you.

Cas came again, somehow, his body twitching and exhausted but somehow still thrusting. He heard Yasahiro moan again, felt Yasa's cock twitch inside him. The spirits said thank you, and the gift of their thanks amplified the pleasure sweeping through Cas, sweeping through Yasahiro. They cried out again and again and again until the spirits were finished and their sweat-slick bodies collapsed, Cas sliding to the floor beside Yasahiro's prone body. In the dying ghost light their exhausted eyes met, and Cas managed a smile.

"My Hiro..." he said and stuck out his tongue, his last action before the darkness dropped fully and he was lost to sweet and dreamless sleep.

Cas winced as he sat down in the passenger's side of the car, pulled his computer to his lap.

"You sure about this?" Rina asked, voice skeptical. Cas sighed, nodded.

"People will say it's just a stunt, you know?" she said. "The public fight, then getting back together. People will think it's just a plot twist you planned ahead of time."

"Let them," Cas said, looked up to see Yasahiro walking his bike over. The investigation was a complete success, and Cas could almost taste the views they'd get, the interviews people would demand, the new jobs, the new places they'd go. Together.

"You said we actually captured the ghosts?" Cas asked, finding the feed from his vest camera and punching it up. Things were confused at first, the confrontation with the shadows. It looked like a bad movie effect, but there it was, the swirling darkness. And then the confusion of pressing and releasing and being tossed to the side, pointing vaguely up. But it did capture the glowing figures that appeared. It was...amazing. This would be huge. Proof.

"I think that should be enough to convince some people," Rina said. "Though the skeptics will still want some sort of additional proof. It is a weird angle, after all." Cas sighed.

"You said the other camera didn't capture anything?" he asked, and Yasahiro finally arrived, nodded in Rina's direction before positioning himself to be able to see over Cas' shoulder. Cas felt a hand land gently on his shoulder, felt the heat still lingering there, like whatever magic they had worked last night was still flowing through them. Which really, he wouldn't have minded at all. There have to be some benefits to being a ghost hunter, right?

"Well, I said that it probably wouldn't be useful..." she said, and Cas squinted, looked up at her to see that she wasn't meeting his gaze, that her face looked a little flushed.

"Wait, what's on that video, then?" he asked, checking for it on his computer but not finding it. "Where is it?"

"Oh, well I figured because it wouldn't be useful, that I'd just hold onto it," she said, and Cas flushed a deep red even as Yasahiro broke out laughing.

"I'm wiping your hard drive," Cas said, reaching into the back to where she kept her computer, at which Yasahiro only laughed harder and Rina cleared her throat. Cas turned back to see her holding a flash drive, smiling devilishly. Cas tried to stand, cursed as the pain in his ass and computer on his lap hampered him.

"Give that here," he demanded, but Rina took a step back and shook her head.

"At least give us a copy, then," Yasahiro said, and Cas growled at them both as they joined together in laughter. It was going to be an insufferable trip to their next assignment, especially with only two brownies left in the tray. He looked up at Yasahiro, at those brown eyes and soft lips and hard body. And somehow his annoyance disappeared, and he shook his head and then joined in as well, their voices rising together into the air over what had once been a prison of sorts for the souls of the dead trapped within, and which, now, could be anything at all.

At the Carousel Stop

Trish DeVene

*D*espite the plush chair's comfort, Mrs. Sanchez sat at its edge, her fingers half in her purse, prepared to grab at something any minute. Working mom, Patrick thought. Always ready to move to the next thing that needed doing.

"No kids?" he asked. She'd insisted on a two-bedroom, but claimed her kids were grown and out of the house. He asked again because when she'd entered his office, she'd been looking behind her as if someone were following—or like she wanted to be sure they stay put.

Besides that he'd smelled cannabis when they'd spoken outdoors—though he had to admit he didn't now that they sat together in the office. He'd had a moment's doubt; maybe she was sneaking in a boyfriend, a dealer. But she was clean, neat, and pleasant, if a little nervous. She would be working and coming home to sleep. An easy tenant.

Pushing the apartment key across the desk, he smiled. He'd rather welcome her than be suspicious. "Welcome, Mrs. Sanchez. I hope you like it here."

As she reached for the key, she shot a quick glance over her shoulder, then looked back apologetically. "I thought—"

"It's the glass case," he said. "You probably saw my reflection." Decorative cherry wood trimmed the curio cabinet, and chopped his reflection in half, but he saw himself sitting tall, his complexion warmly Irish. He'd gotten his hair trimmed close and neat. He felt presentable. It had been a rough week, but wasn't it always?

She stood. He almost wished she'd had a kid or two, a college guy maybe who'd laze around the small pool—glistening sleekness soaking sun, legs spread casually either side of the lounge chair. Patrick pushed the thought away and extended his hand.

"Welcome, then."

"You have a lovely smile," she said. "It's in your eyes." With that she left. Had he been smiling? In the curio cabinet he saw only a carousel of unicorns. And that reminded him that the collection needed dusting. He was the one who had said, "Don't throw them away," and now he stared at them every day, pointed reminders.

*H*e'd told Mrs. Sanchez he'd fix the leak under her sink in the morning, but her plea for immediate help had felt fragile, her voice quivering. Patrick glanced over at his dad asleep on the rented hospital bed. It raised and lowered and made life a little easier. His sister sat head-bent over her crossword puzzles. The doctors said not to worry about her eyesight, that the concentration was good for her condition. It reined her thoughts, kept her steady.

Patrick's ham with cheddar sandwich still oozed with melting cheese. Taking a bite of the pickle, he shifted his napkin to cover the plate. It could wait, he guessed.

In the chill dusk, he followed the narrow sidewalk to the Sanchez apartment. Sure enough, there it was—already he smelled sweet burning weed. He rarely smoked anymore. Anymore? Who was he kidding? Adult responsibilities hit him full force when his mom died. Still, it smelled good, like relaxation.

Relax. Patrick stopped at the whisper. Of course, it was only the breeze playing tricks with his tired mind, but the smell of weed had grown stronger. Mrs. Sanchez's front window was lit with a small lamp, and the spare room was shaded but cracked to an inch of darkness. Patrick knocked and immediately the locks clicked open.

Her smile, apologetic and grateful, relaxed him as much as any drink or other high could. "I understand," he assured her. "Even a slow drip can puddle quickly."

Nodding, her gaze flicked to the hall instead of the kitchen.

Patrick shifted the toolbox to his other hand. Someone else was there. He felt it. Not in sound, and he no longer smelled the smoke, but...a breathing presence. He swore he heard a laugh.

"This way," she said, pointing to the open kitchen. A counter divided the room, and on it was one plate, one glass, and a paperback book propped open.

In the sink, one plastic cup caught the slow drip. Okay, there were certainly no signs of another. He was imagining things. As he set the toolbox down, she jumped at the clank, then wrung her hands.

"Are you okay, Mrs. Sanchez?"

Again, that relieved smile. "Yes, yes. Thank you for coming." She had already emptied the cabinet and he wedged his upper body inside and shined the flashlight. "Do you mind..." she started. "Do you mind if I run to the supermarket?"

Already he heard her unsnapping her purse, jangling keys. "No problem," he said.

As she moved, shadows played over his legs. Too much movement for one person, one slight person, he thought. He tapped the trap. It would need replacing. The front door clanged closed. All the doors in the place shut solidly. He liked them heavy and secure.

Again a shadow shifted; Patrick scooted out fast.

No one. But there was that smell again. "What the—" Quietly setting the wrench on the counter, Patrick peered down the hall. Dark doorways stretched tall and silent. A tingle of fear made his dick twitch, and he rubbed himself, then looked over his shoulder.

He respected people's privacy. He didn't want to pry.

About to turn back, he heard the scratch, like a match striking. Light flickered from the spare bedroom. "Hello?" he called.

A breath exhaled. A small laugh.

Okay, he'd given warning. Fingers trailing the cool wall, Patrick headed toward the bedroom, then stopped in the doorway. "Hello?" Another long exhale. Definitely someone smoking. "I'm fixing the sink. I didn't realize someone was home."

No answer except a subtle moan, a slight shifting. Another tingling twitch and he felt himself growing hard. What the fuck? Fear had never given him a hard on… There, the laugh again.

Enough. He owned this place. He had a right. Patrick flipped on the light.

On the bed still made, a young guy lay slightly propped on pillows, joint between his fingers. A grin crooked his lush, full lips. "Hola," the guy said and laughed.

"Hol…" The word barely whispered from Patrick's mouth. The guy was gorgeous. The holy-shit-kind of hot. His thin body lay relaxed and inviting; soft jeans rippled over his legs, zipper bunched with a swell. He wore a tank tee, pin-striped, and the smooth subtle muscling of his arms, the shine of clavicle hinted at what was beneath.

"I didn't realize someone was here," Patrick explained.

The guy's face was smoky angelic, sultry black lashes and brows, smooth brown skin, contoured like graceful hills and valleys. His eyes flashed with a wicked dare. "Didn't you?" he asked.

Rising slightly, he reached out to share his smoke. The shirt gaped, a hint of his bronze-shined chest, a shadowed dip…

Patrick's throat caught. He didn't speak, only took the offered joint and toked. Then hurriedly, he gave it back. This wasn't something he could get involved in. He had to leave.

The guy flopped back, one arm outstretched as if he'd abandoned himself to the moment. His eyes narrowed, hazing as his other hand ran down his stomach and stopped at the beltline. "Relax," he said, then the outstretched arm drew back, long, slim fingers to his lips for another hit. He willowed. He seemed to drift.

"Are you her son?"

The guy stared, unmoving, though his body's energy pulsed like it was setting Patrick's heartbeat. He could almost taste that warm sheen of tight skin, feel the ruffled black silk of his hair.

"Take off your shirt," the guy said. It felt like a lazy command, what might come from a person who expects his desires to be fulfilled.

For a moment, Patrick looked down at himself. He was tall and lean and in good shape still despite his family obligations. He was hard already. No denying that. But this was exactly the kind of guy he had vowed to stay away from. No more one-night stands, no more using—

"Unbuckle the pants." The second command startled him. The guy hadn't moved, but stared at the ceiling, almost as if bored with what he asked. His fingers slid button from hole on those soft-cloud blue jeans. He unzipped, sending a metallic shiver through Patrick. The swelling he held within ached for release.

"Your mom will be back," he said, but the guy's hand dug into his pants, stroking. Jesus, he wanted to part those casual legs, raise them and dive into this man. Reaching back, Patrick swung the bedroom door closed. Then stripping off his shirt, he put a knee on the bed between legs that pathed to exactly what Patrick needed.

He ran his hands up the guy's jeans, thumbs along his inner thighs. As his stomach concaved, Patrick buried his face in it. He moaned, raised the pin-striped shirt, and licked the suck and quiver. The guy arched to him. Just a slip of fabric away, his dick throbbed beneath Patrick's chin. Patrick licked below the brief's elastic, then with both hands yanked the jeans from pointed, narrow hips.

In his periphery, he saw the man's toned, silken arm drift back across the bed, the joint snuffed in a jade-green ashtray. And he heard an exhale that sounded like a laugh. A hand pressed the back of his head, inching him down. As he pulled at the elastic waistband, the guy's swollen cock popped to his lips. This was what he wanted. This was what he vowed to forget.

He wrapped his lips around the tip then thrust down, wanting to choke on it, to swallow him. He grabbed the guy's tiny tight ass and pulled up.

Outside the room, a door clanked shut.

"Shit!" Patrick jumped up and snatched his shirt from the floor. The guy started stroking his cock still wet with Patrick's saliva. As he stretched his head back, his neck was desire elongated, thick with need, a phallus like the one reddening in his hand. "Your mom," Patrick whispered, pulling the shirt over his head.

"Relax," the guy whispered, and his climax shot over that glorious sheen of skin.

*P*eering out the bedroom, Patrick saw the thin strip of light under the bathroom door. He had a chance of escape. He glanced back in the room, but the guy was no longer on the bed. What the fuck? Where did he go?

The toilet flushed. No way would Patrick blow this chance of escape. He skirted through the hall, grabbed his wrench from the counter, and wedged back under the sink. He let the wrench clang loudly as if he'd been working all along, hadn't heard her, didn't know how much life was moving about the apartment.

He was sweating. He imagined his dad on the front couch calling, Patrick, Patrick, wanting his pills, wanting his water, and his sister ducking deeper and deeper into her crosswords.

Mrs. Sanchez's shadow draped his leg again. He tightened a nut and peeked out with a smile. "All fixed." He'd have to replace the trap but he'd come back for that. His hands were shaky. He hadn't eaten.

"I'll need to come back to replace some parts, but for now the leak should hold." Her eyes were wide with question and he sensed it wasn't about the leak. "I didn't realize you had a guest staying. Your son?"

Mrs. Sanchez checked that instinct to glance over her shoulder. "My son died five years ago."

"I'm sorry." Patrick hated that the words didn't sound sincere, but she was too nervous to be telling the truth. Packing up his toolbox, he watched her shoulders relax as she looked around the room. Her body loosened. When she turned back to him, her smile was warm.

"Thank you," she said. "So very much." She reached for his hand. "I will bake you buñuelos de viento...with custard. Fritters," she clarified.

Patrick laughed. "No need. This is my job." She looked like she might embrace him. What had happened? Was it relief that he didn't press her about the extra tenant? Could he be a lover and she was embarrassed to say so? No. It wasn't that. Patrick was sure the guy was her son. He felt so sure of it. Where was he now? Standing just within the doorframe, out of sight? His pants still open, that glossed stomach rippling with suppressed laughter?

Were his eyes bright, those warm brown eyes, gold-flecked with knowing? Knowing that Patrick still wanted him?

She held his hand in both of hers a moment. "He's dead," she said. "My son. But he'll rest now. He'll rest."

He could only nod. Strange that he had no sense of that other presence anymore. The room did feel lighter. Or maybe empty. He nodded again to her. "Good night, then, Mrs. Sanchez."

"Los buñuelos. I'll have them for you tomorrow."

He wasn't going to argue. The door was in reach, and he wanted to hear it clang behind him as he left.

Sometimes a latch's click, the bang of a door echoed long into night's dreaming. Patrick couldn't sleep. The TV that held his dad through the night, flashed through Patrick's bedroom. He didn't dare close the door, though he stroked himself and wanted to throw the covers off for the heat building in him.

He wanted to sneak out, tap at that flat dark window where inside a smoky angel probably laughed to himself at Patrick's gaping stupidity. He wanted to pin him down to the bed, and this time finish. He gripped his dick hard and rubbed quicker. And with the image of that neck stretched back in ecstasy, he shot his release. Fuck, he wanted that man.

Drying himself with his shorts, he turned to his side. Since his mom died and he'd taken over family care, he'd turned to one-night stands, often no names. The same type, the ones whose eyes would say, "I'm no good for you. Do you dare?" Yes, because that's what he needed. And yet...when it was finished, when he turned to his side, an ache swelled in his stomach, up his esophagus. He'd feel sick and wonder if this was the rest of his life.

Like the unicorn carousels his mom had left behind, these small pleasures went round his life, encased, inaccessible, yet always coming around to tempt and tease. Magic. That's what she said she loved about unicorns—they represented childhood wonder, belief in the impossible, magic. Sometimes real life sucked all that away.

How would those slender, brown musician's fingers feel on his body, trickling up his thigh? *He'll rest now*—he heard Mrs. Sanchez's words like a whisper outside his thoughts. What had she meant? *Her son was dead five years.*

Ghosts. Did she believe he was a spirit, unsettled, lingering on earth?

The thought scratched at each door he closed in his mind. Where had the guy gone? Was he real, there on the bed? Of course, he was. He'd spoken; he'd laughed and gasped and shot semen in a lively stream.

Patrick gripped his swelling cock again. Jesus, he had to forget this guy. He rolled to his stomach; he imagined the pillow with a ruffle of black silk hair, the cool cotton was warm plush lips. Oh that grin, that careless wild tease.

*A*fternoon sun hazed weakly through the office blinds, and Patrick turned the home monitor to face him. His sister had gone off on the bus five hours ago, and his dad had been quiet since. He'd checked on him three times. Morphine sleep usually had him moaning and turning, but he'd been breathing easy. There were days like that sometimes, and Patrick leaned back in the chair, feet up on the desk, and imagined a scenario where he knocked on the Sanchez apartment door and the guy answered sleepily, swinging back to let Patrick in.

The office door chimed, snapping his feet to the floor. "Good morning!" He sounded too cheerful. *And* it was afternoon. "I mean—"

She was back to wringing her hands. "That leak," she said. "You had parts to replace?"

That son no longer at rest? he thought, immediately regretting the meanness. "Has it started up again?"

She shook her head. "No, no, but you said..."

What did she want from him? Standing, Patrick walked around the desk and leaned against it. "Mrs. Sanchez, is something…are you afraid of something? Someone?"

She touched the beveled wooden trim of the curio cabinet. "You collect unicorns?"

Patrick laughed. "No. No. They were my mom's."

She looked at him, startled. "I'm sorry." Then she returned her gaze to the cabinet, stooping to look more closely at the myriad forms of fantasy. "The leak doesn't usually come back?" she asked, keeping her eyes on the cabinet.

He laughed again. "Um, no, not if I do the job right."

Then she turned and her eyes were bright again. She smiled. "Good. You're a caretaker, aren't you? I knew you could do it."

He didn't like the implications in that, the crazy thoughts that crossed his mind, but he let it go. "I'm going to work," she said. "I'll be gone till evening."

This was an obvious invitation. She barely had the key in her car door, and already he was standing outside the apartment, smelling that sweet smoke.

*I*t wasn't until he was standing in the middle of the front room that Patrick realized he'd entered without ringing the buzzer. But there wasn't supposed to be anyone home, right? Did he hear that sarcastic laugh already? That cocky assurance from a guy who probably hadn't even left his bed?

Ghost. The word whispered in Patrick's head. Part of him believed it possible, the other remembered how tactile-tangible that molten body had been. He smoothed his shirt, his chest hard, his stomach firm. His cock twitched with pleasure. On the counter he saw a plate of pastries. The buñuelos, of course.

"Hello?" he called.

Nothing.

The smell of smoke grew stronger. Patrick stripped off his shirt. Fuck this guy with his lazy tease. There'd be no commands this time except from him. He strode the short hall like he was seizing the room, maybe a country, a continent, the famed and fabled...

Patrick stopped in the doorway. There he lay. Same clothes, same pose. A burnished brown landscape, a midnight sky, those half-closed eyes hazed with seduction. He toked.

"Hola," he said and laughed.

"I didn't realize..." He stopped on realizing they'd done this before.

"Didn't you?"

The tingling throb in his dick twisted to a twinge of fear. Patrick's stomach went hollow. "What are you?"

Rising on one elbow, the guy reached out to share his smoke. There—the shirt gaping, the tempting hint of bronze-shined chest...Patrick's throat caught. Again. He didn't take the offering. Instead he touched the guy's legs, a hand on each shin. Solid. Skinny. They parted further at Patrick's touch.

He flopped back, one arm outstretched, eyes hazing as his other hand trickled over the tight stomach that caved with his exhale. "Relax," he said, and took another hit.

That prick of fear sparked a new tingling throb. Real or not, this guy's thighs under his hands were taut, his hips arching to Patrick's fingered approach.

"I'm fucking you this time," Patrick said.

"Take off your shirt."

"It's already off," he answered and bit the glistening skin at his hipbone. He pushed the pin-stripe shirt up and licked up the lean, satin chest. He tongued his nipple, and a gasp startled him. The guy's head was thrown back, plush lips parted, and his hips pushed against Patrick's.

It wouldn't be exactly the same as last time. Not exactly. Patrick unbuckled his pants and pushed the guy's hand away as he tried to undo his own. Quickly, he scooted up on his knees, straddling this sultry, smoking, cocksure kid. He fisted his own cock and stroked it against the guy's stomach. The body trapped beneath him undulated with each struggling gasp as he tried to undo himself, to repeat the same masturbation.

Stroking harder, sliding his cock against the burnished land beneath him, Patrick caught those full parted lips in his own. The fingers that still held the burning weed loosed their hold. Empty, they flexed, open to air. Driving his tongue into him, suffocating his mouth, Patrick felt a crazy spasm through his chest, a rough coil down his throat. *Pain.* The guy's nose against his own, the radiant ball of his cheekbone against Patrick's cheek, the lashes fluttering—it ached in him. He thrust against the guy's stomach and splattered his semen over a land he could bury himself in.

Did he know the pain of need? Did he feel it?

"Unbuckle—" The guy started, and Patrick kissed him hard to shut it off.

It was the same, all the same. Again, another climax ultimately heading to nothing. Worse, what did he have this time? A ghost? Was this guy even real?

Patrick rose to his knees, and the guy finished his sentence. "...the belt."

He secured his buckle instead, and watched as the ghost-man unbuttoned, unzipped, reached inside. He stared at the ceiling and stroked. But the other hand was empty now. Palm up, empty.

The unicorn. Patrick suddenly wanted that one radiant stallion unicorn, the one up on its hind legs. He ran out, not waiting for the guy to come. Before he finished, he needed something else in his hands.

It was crazy, he told himself as he miscued the key in the office lock, tried again, banged the door open, and raided the curio cabinet he'd left to dust.

He hadn't wanted her collection, the cliché of unicorns, the ste-reotypes. "Leave them to their jaded vision," she'd say. "I'd rather believe in magic." He used to write stories about locked towers and twisting dungeon stairs and magic keys to unlock it all.

Rushing back into the Sanchez apartment, for a second he stopped again in the front room. The house settled quietly under half-drawn shades. What if he had finished? What if Patrick entered to have him say, "Hola"?

With renewed trepidation, he peered in the room.

It was empty.

*F*uck. Patrick propped his dad up on the extra pillow and broke off a piece of the grilled cheese sandwich to place it between his lips, glossed with Vaseline.

The guy wasn't real, his mind kept saying. But how did one believe that? And what kind of joke was life playing on him? He'd had no resolve. He'd slipped into another mistaken escape through sex. And this time it was even less real. Just like the guy reliving the same event, Patrick was trapped.

"There's a guy," he said to his dad.

Tired, his dad's eyes raised slowly. He chewed deliberately, then looked at the TV tray filled with medicines, moisturizers, the nebulizer. Patrick had placed the unicorn carousel there. Why leave them all trapped in the curio?

His dad smiled faintly, a warm smile. Slumping, Patrick smiled too. "I hope it's okay, Dad. I gave two unicorns to the Mezner kids and one to Lily down in 109."

Opening his mouth for another bite of cheese, his dad closed his eyes and settled his head back again. He chewed as if savoring the only meal that he seemed to want anymore.

A shadow crossed the bed. "What guy?" His sister startled him; she walked as quietly as her crosswords undid themselves.

Relinquishing, Patrick let the emotion come. "Someone I want to help." He closed his eyes. "Or maybe I want him to help me." He pulled the stallion unicorn from his pocket. "I want to give him this one."

"Oh, Patrick," she said with a smirk. "He'll think you're silly and pathetic." Then she kissed his head and ruffled the short fluff of hair he wished was lying on a pillow beside midnight's lush and wondrous, long-lashed dream. Yes, he was being silly, ridiculous.

But he had to try. Once more. "Nadia, can you watch dad while I go fix a leak?" he asked. Already she was at the table, bent to the crossword. She would be no help. He twirled the stallion in his hands. *Round and round, never stopping...* His dad's hand touched Patrick's. Then one finger tapped the unicorn and his dad nodded, then closed his eyes again.

"*H*ola."

God, he couldn't seize him again, not with that vicious lust he'd felt before. It was near evening. Mrs. Sanchez would be returning. Patrick just wanted to change something.

Those sensual fingers clipped the smoking joint. The body sighed into the bed with invitation. Patrick let the scene play. He removed his shirt when commanded. But when those brown eyes fixed on him with that clever dare, when he extended the smoke, Patrick flicked it out and took the guy's...*the ghost's* wrists. Kneeling on the bed, he pinned him. There would be only a kiss.

"Didn't you?" broke from the ghost-man's lips, but Patrick ignored the words and feathered his eyelids with kisses. He gently trailed across his temple, cheek against cheek. That black silk hair brushed Patrick's forehead and made his throat catch again. The wrists in his grip grew hot. The body arched against him, pushing to be released.

"I want you to stay," Patrick said.

Gasps replaced the words he might say, his body pumping against Patrick in a frantic search for what it knew. Patrick held him and tenderly kissed his cheekbones, chin, whispering, "Live, move on."

One violent thrust, and Patrick's hands went cold. He lay face-down on an empty bed.

"No!" He stifled the cry in the pillow. Then undoing his pants, with manic frustration he pumped into his hand. He collapsed, feeling the sticky spread beneath him. "Come back."

The room was silent and smelled like lemon furniture polish. His left hand ached, and Patrick saw that he'd been gripping the unicorn. He didn't know when he'd taken it out of his pocket. Scooting off the bed, he placed the unicorn on the nightstand beside the ashtray. Then moved it into the ashtray. He checked the drawers and found ten rolled joints in a row. That much was real? Was his mother trying to sustain him, or did he haunt her with demands?

Scooping all remnants from the drawer, Patrick noted the darkened windows. She'd be home. There was a semen stain in the center of the bed.

"Come back," he said to the empty room.

*M*rs. Sanchez set the apartment key and buñuelos on Patrick's office desk. "You're so kind to let me break the lease. I didn't expect—"

"It's not a problem." He didn't want to hear her excuse. He couldn't be angry, not with the sadness in her eyes, the rich sweetness of the dessert she brought, but he wanted to beg her to stay.

"Will it happen again?" he asked.

She stopped at the curio cabinet. "You removed some pieces."

Patrick rounded his desk to look at the dusty outlines of figurines now gone. "Sometimes you have to move on."

She raised large brown eyes to him. They were like her son's, flecked with gold. In them, a touch of innocence, like hope. "You left a figurine in the room."

Patrick only nodded.

"I thought maybe...this time..." She looked at him. "Yes, it will happen again." And then she snapped her purse and walked out.

He picked up the phone to call the cleaning service. He had a wait-list—another tenant would fill the rooms by the weekend. Before the recording answered, Patrick hung up. One more look at the place, maybe he could lie down a moment and soak up the sensual smell of that ghost, the luxurious carnal existence that pulsed hotter than anything Patrick knew in real life. That ghost's stuck existence that felt so much like his own life.

He fit the key in the lock and sighed. It was pointless. His life wasn't going to change. He was stuck in this place, while the carousel went round. He almost turned back when he heard a sound inside. Like a cabinet closing. He turned the key. A click.

Inside, a plate clinked on the counter.

His heartbeat sped. "Hello?" he called.

"Hola."

No throb in his dick, Patrick nearly pissed himself in the doorway.

He glanced to the parking lot—Mrs. Sanchez's car was gone. She was gone. She moved on. What the hell had he got himself into?

He stepped into the front room and looked down the hall. But then he heard another cabinet close. In the kitchen, a shadow moved. The ghost stood, a butter knife in one hand, and a grin on his face. The unicorn sat on the counter, in its ecstatic joy pawing the air.

"Hola," Patrick said. He waited, while those gold-brown eyes soaked into him.

"I was hungry," the ghost said.

Relief rushed through Patrick. No, it was joy. Pure, thrilling joy.

He really stood there, those full lips spreading to a wide white smile. Stood there, bare-chested, his warm brown skin slightly moist as if he'd just showered. "God," Patrick whispered, approaching the form that held the knife with no food on the plate before him. Could he eat food?

"Are you a figment of my imagination? A ghost?" His black hair was damp, ruffled, cut neat at his neck, his shoulder a slick shine as if the sun nestled under his skin. Such beautiful skin, polished and aflame.

"Are you real?" he asked coming up behind him.

Those sun-shoulders shrugged. "I'm here. I'm hungry."

But was the hunger real? There was no food on the plate. Patrick touched his shoulder, then put his lips to the back of his neck. Touching him was diving into sunlit silk, or flying under raven's wing, and yet so sensuously human, roiling with carnal desire. Patrick kissed down the long spine, his hands following the elegant taper to his waist. Hungry? He was starved for this man.

Kissing along his belt line, Patrick ran his hands over the pliant jeans, over his knees, up his inner thighs. His tiny ass tightened, and Patrick rested his face against it—breathing, just taking a luxurious breath, and letting it shiver down.

As his fingers rose to the zipper, pressing the hard swell of this hungry being, an ache in his chest said, *This one can't go.* Patrick had to ask, "Will you stay?"

On the counter, the slim, deft fingers shifted the knife between thumb and forefinger, as if grasping a joint. *No, please no.* Patrick put his forehead against the small of his back. The knife clinked. The hand took his and pushed it harder over his cock that wanted to burst past biting zipper.

The ghost-man gasped, his other hand gripping the counter. Oh god, that hard tingling need whipped up Patrick's throat. He nearly cried out as he ran his tongue up the man's lustrous back. He bit his neck as his hand was crushed against the counter, the ghost grinding his hard cock into it.

Catching the zipper, Patrick loosed him, and fell to his knees again, stripping down the pants, nibbling his ass, as he pulled the jeans off, one foot, the next. Each movement was a treasure. The taut calf muscles, the tensing as he ran his hands back up the inner thighs.

He tongued the round half-moons of this beauty, down his crack, licking for the deeper smells of sex. And his gaze rose to his sculpted elegance. Would he stay?

"Do it." The voice this time was hoarse and awake in its demand. With a grin of pure willingness, Patrick dove back to the caverns, tasting the warm moist sex of him. He flicked his tongue along balls that contracted at the touch, roiling too with the production of seed.

Then, stretching back, the guy raised both arms high over his head. Patrick grabbed the cock that twitched against the counter, then undid his own pants and stood body against body.

Stretched back, hands reaching—this ghost was the stallion unicorn ready to seize the world again.

Hands cupping his rib cage, Patrick turned the smoky angel, sunlit and clear now, to face him. His gold-brown eyes, hazed with desire, held a glint of humor, a bit of dare. He'd be a tease, this one, yes. Patrick kissed down his nose, pausing at his parted lips.

"Have I gone crazy finally? Are you a figment—?"

Those white teeth bit Patrick's lip. "Let's fuck." Another command from the figment, the dream, the ghost, the man.

The apartment would remain vacant in the ledgers but would be filled with a new life stirring awake. He heard the smack of lubricant. How did a ghost...? No time to consider. The guy turned Patrick to face the counter. "Unbuckle the pants," he said.

Same words. No. No, it couldn't be the same scene, the residual life of a spirit trapped. No. This was a man meant to walk with purpose, to grasp and conquer and thrill the world.

Teeth nibbled at his neck; a warm tongue tickled his ear. Then a laugh. "Oh, I'll conquer, all right," he said, and shoved Patrick's pants to his knees.

His slick cock slid down Patrick's ass. He played the tip at the opening, circling, and he grabbed Patrick's dick, stroking. Pressure. Tentative. Then a little more. Patrick bit his lip, both hands tight on the counter edge. What was he waiting for?

He thrust into the guy's hand. Still, the pressure teased his ass. Thrusting again, Patrick pushed back into the guy. "Fuck. Do it."

In a shatter of tingling pain, of exquisite opening, he entered.

Striking back against him, meeting the rhythm, Patrick stared at the unicorn stallion riding the air. This was letting go; this was racing with a world out of his control. Magic—did he believe in it?

Behind him a beauty that wrung the heart thrust with abandoned ecstasy into him. He was going to explode and he didn't know if when it ended the ghost would be there still.

He heard each grunt, each skin slap, memorized the rhythm of his breaths. "Stay," moaned out of him as he shot hard into the stroking hand. His arms weakened against the last hard pounding, the ghost-man's final thrust, stilled to liquid pulse. Inside him. The ghost's arms wrapped his waist. Silk hair ruffled his back.

He was here. Jesus, he was still here. Patrick dropped to his elbows, bent over the counter. Did he dare turn?

"I kinda like this place," the ghost said. His fingers tickled up Patrick's chest then tweaked his nipple. There was that laugh again.

What had he gotten himself into?

Patrick turned.

There he stood, glistening now with a thin coat of sweat. Dusk-angel, morning demon—Patrick didn't know what he was. But his eyes glimmered with cocky assurance, and it seemed like he wanted to stay. God, *what* had he gotten himself into?

Beauty, mysterious and magical—the guy stepped back and put those tempting slim fingers on the slip of his lip-biting hips. "Really," he said. "I'm hungry."

Birthday Boy

T. P. Watcher

*I*an knocked on my door at about three. He never used the bell for some reason, and the knocking nearly woke up my dog, Pippin.

I opened the inside door and gestured for him to come in through the storm door. I was just finishing up a call, and he just half-waved as he moved past me to find a seat on the couch.

"Happy birthday!" I said after I'd hung up. "How's it been so far?"

He shrugged. "Been in school all day. Mom and dad wouldn't let me skip."

That didn't surprise me. Eve and Mike had been drawn to each other when we were in college together because they were both free spirits, but once they'd had kids, they each had shown a surprisingly strong hand in child-rearing. Ian wasn't exactly repressed, but he was expected to fulfill his responsibilities, which included a number of chores, keeping himself looking (and smelling) presentable, and doing his best in school. Not showing up just because he was turning sixteen definitely didn't fit their definition of "doing his best." On the other hand, he was given a fair amount of trust and freedom alike, and he didn't hide from them the fact that he experimented with being a healthy teenager. They allowed him to make his own mistakes within reason, and expected him to clean up his own messes when possible.

"That's what parents are for," I said in sympathy. "Got any plans for tonight?"

He shook his head. "Not really, it's a school night. Mom's going to make a cake, but I told her to wait until the weekend when I can have friends over to eat it with."

"And get presents from." I laughed. "Speaking of which, I had three ideas about what to give you today, but only one of them is both legal and mind-blowing. Well, might be mind-blowing if you pick right. That would be going to a movie," I said. My heart sped up a tiny bit, because I'd been rehearsing these lines and giving a lot of thought as to how the conversation might go. Like over a year and half, in truth. I tried to sound casual.

"And what are the other two?" he asked, right on cue.

"Well, the illegal, mind-blowing one would be to smoke some of my weed with you. I've always said I would when I thought you were mature enough. The other one is also illegal, but not mind-blowing…just blowing, really. As in me, blowing you."

He was quiet for a moment, a long moment, as my heart pounded and his eyes didn't meet mine. Then he looked up at me and asked, "Do I have to pick just one?"

I smiled. "Having a hard time choosing?"

He shuffled his feet. "Well I could tell my parents you gave me the first one," he said, "but I was thinking that the second one would make the third one way better."

"Why don't we go into the bedroom and get more comfortable?" I asked. "I think we can work something out."

He nodded, his face expressionless as he started towards the one room I had really wanted to get him into for oh-so-long. Without any obvious gestures, he managed to leave his shoes behind as he did so. I followed him into the room, where he just stood for a moment, then turned to face me. "Where should I sit?" he asked.

"Bed's fine, or desk chair, I said, pointing out the only options other than the floor. I didn't have the kind of bedroom with an antechamber or sitting room attached, like those guys (and kids!) who always seem to be incredibly well off in erotic fiction stories. Usually they got their money when a tragic accident killed their parents, but apparently the massive inheritance was enough to get them over their grief, because they are inevitably screwing like rabbits by the third paragraph in. I just had a full-size bed, dresser, computer desk with chair, and a little nightstand. The dresser actually was my inheritance; it's big, antique, and means if I ever move again I'm going to need new friends, because I think I lost a couple when I got into this single-bedroom apartment.

Ian dropped onto the edge of the mattress with a little bounce, and I heard a barely-uttered "nice" in reaction to the spring. I took the desk, and pulled out the wooden box I keep my greenery and equipment in.

"I know this isn't your first time with this stuff," I said, "but get a whiff of this." I opened the tin and passed it to him. He took a tentative sniff, and his eyes widened a bit. Then, he looked closely.

"It's got orange hairs," he said.

I smiled. "Look closer."

He did, and his voice raised in pitch when he asked, "Is that really purple?"

"It is."

I went through the process of breaking some up and rolling it into a joint, taking my time and adding lots of flourishes. I was showing off for fun, but also to give myself time to calm down. All my hopes, all my dreams, sitting on my bed and awaiting my desires.

As I was rolling, he yawned and stretched, raising his arms above his head and his shirt above his navel. I was so captivated by that three-inch band of smooth, tight abdomen that I stopped what I was doing, so he noticed when he was done, and laughed. "You sure it's me getting the present, and not you?" he asked.

Snapping out of it, I finished the rolling operation, my face warm. "The perfect deal is the one where everyone gets what he wants," I said. "Have you smoked a joint before? Or a cigarette? I hope no cigarettes, but just tell me."

Ian shook his head. "I've just tried bowls and bongs," he said.

"Okay, this might feel a little more harsh than you're used to, but I'll get some choke-stop and it won't be a big deal." I went to the kitchen and snatched a couple of glasses and a bottle of soda from the fridge. "You ready?" He nodded, again with an unreadable face. He never had much of a facial expression.

I bit off one end, and lit the other, puffing to get it going, and inspecting it for side-burn. Satisfied, I took a hit and held it as I explained what he should do.

"Take a smaller hit than you normally would, and suck in plenty of air after it. Get used to how it feels, and you should be able to avoid a coughing fit. This isn't a contest measuring how big a hit you take. If anything, you should be seeing how long you can hold it in." With that, I slowly exhaled.

"I think I get it," he said, reaching for the still-smoldering joint. "Size doesn't matter, just how long I can last."

Somehow I managed to choke just then, and needed to take a drink. He laughed. "Actually even how long you last doesn't really matter, because you can do it again and again, all night if you want."

He made it through his first two hits like a champ, then got overconfident on the third, and started to cough. It didn't last long, though. "If you cough, you get off," I said.

"I sure hope so," he said. "This stuff is definitely making me feel really good."

"You ready to try something more...adventurous?" I asked.

He raised an eyebrow. "Like?"

"Ever see someone do a shotgun?" He shook his head, and I smiled. "You'll like this. I'm going to put the lit end of the joint in my mouth, and you put yours on the other end, only don't actually hold it in your lips. When I nod, I'll start blowing out, and you start sucking in your hit."

He looked puzzled but following my instructions. I think he understood as soon as he realized I was pushing a steady stream of smoke out for him and took in as much as he could. He was so close I could feel the warmth of his face on my own.

Ian held it for only about ten seconds but let it out slowly as he stretched out on the bed.

"You're feeling no pain," I said.

"I'm supposed to be feeling more than that," he said.

My pulse quickened. "Since as you said, you're also the present, I'm going to unwrap you completely," I said, trying to keep my voice from shaking.

"Completely?" he squeaked. "How come?"

"The more I get to see, the more fun I have," I said. "The more I see, the less I have to imagine, so the more attention I can pay to what I'm doing. Is that going to be a problem?"

"Nah, makes sense. Go for it."

I did. Never, ever, second-guess a boy when he has given consent. Sometimes it does not get repeated. I stepped quickly over to the bed, put my knees on either side of his hips, and lifted up his t-shirt, prompting him to lift his arms to get it the rest of the way off. I knew there was a dusting of brown hairs under his arms, but my eyes lingered, as it was finally safe to look closely. Besides that and the faintest hint of something above his lip, no other hairs disturbed the skin from face to waist. He had the body of a sixteen-year-old whose metabolism was adapted to a mostly sedentary lifestyle; none of the muscle definition of a true athlete but lean enough that his ribs could be counted with my fingers, just not my eyes. Not that I was ready to touch him, yet. I wanted to take a moment to just…look.

"What?" he said, growing self-conscious under my gaze.

"I was trying to get your nipples hard with my mind," I replied.

"You like hard nipples?" he asked.

"Not as much as I like making nipples hard," I answered. "Watch." I moved my hips back so I could comfortably descend upon the left one without banging into his chin. Looking him in the eye, I stuck out my tongue, and lightly touched it in the very center. Then, while trying to look at his face, I slowly moved it around in circles before withdrawing, only to exhale onto it, so the cooling air would do the trick. "See?" I said. "You could cut glass. That was fun."

"But that's only one," he said, his voice slightly lower in volume, as well as pitch.

"So it is," I said, before moving to give the right the same treatment. "I could do that for hours."

"Just the nipples?" he asked, with a hint of whine.

I grinned. "You know what else. You just don't know how long it will take me to get there."

"I know you still owe me a movie," he said. "Unless you want to suck me in the theater?"

Bold boy! I put my thumbs on his hard, moist buttons and rubbed them gently. "When I'm done if you still want more, we can talk about that, but don't hold your breath about me doing that in public."

"You better stop talking, then, if you don't want to have to do that. I expect all of my presents."

I smiled, and gently pushed him back onto the bed. Two can be bold, I thought, as I reached out and gently lowered his zipper. With the back of my fingers, I exerted some exploratory pressure, but came up empty. Then it was his turn to laugh.

"It's not that small. Here, try taking my pants off." He yanked them down himself, ruining my fantasy of slowly disrobing him, and taking his socks along with them. All that remained was a pair of boxers that covered everything but concealed nothing, like a Freudian slip.

"Are those satin?" I asked, and he nodded. They were black with a red flame design; across the front was written the message, "hot stuff." His boner was trying to escape down the left leg but wasn't quite long enough to be visible. I ran my fingers along the satin-covered shaft, which felt to be five or six inches. "Very sexy," I said. "Very hard."

"If you don't do something about it, it's going to stay that way for a long, long time," he said, putting his hands over mine and thrusting. Locking eyes with mine, he said, "I'm just so horny."

I nodded, understanding that his idea of special and mine weren't going to meld. I pulled his boxers downward, and the satin slid from under his ass without him having to lift it. As his cock came free, it lolled to one side.

"Hmm." I said. "I thought it was supposed to smack your belly."

"What?" asked Ian.

"Nothing." I put his dick in my mouth. The bouquet of his balls overcame me with lust as he let out an "Oh!" that told me he definitely wanted this. He spread his legs and clenched his abs hard enough that I did make out some of the muscle under his taut skin. I grabbed his soft, round cheeks in my hands and guided them up as I went down, and as we picked up a rhythm I watched the tight line of his navel advance and retreat before me, with nary a hair anywhere near it but for the brown ones sprouting above the member which presently occupied all of his attention and most of my mouth.

His shaft slid into my throat as smooth as silk, probably because my mouth had been watering over this moment for years. I gently rolled his balls in my hand as I bobbed on his shaft, then switching it up by kissing them before touching my tongue's tip to that of his young cock and watching him flail about as I caught that spot under the head. He wasn't trying to fuck my face: neither did he thrust his hips, nor shove my head down with his hands so caught up was he with the sensations between his legs. I had to do all the work. And work him I did. He wasn't really quite long enough for me to deep throat, but I made sure I got him as far down as he could reach.

"Let me hear you," I said, coming up for air myself. "Let me hear how it feels."

His breathing, already spastic, accelerated a bit before he let out a timid little moan, all but buried in his exhalation. As I sucked him deep, he tried again, and it sounded more like a sex noise. No words but getting a boy to make noise at all after learning to hide evidence of their fapping is progress.

As he got more into it, I put my hands under his ass and pulled him deeper into my mouth. "Oh god," he cried, and I would have smiled but for the cock in my throat. Instead, I moaned around his shaft, and reached a hand around to caress his abs and chest. If that level of intimacy might have bothered him, he was now too far gone to care. In fact, he demonstrated how little he cared for decorum by lifting his legs up and putting his feet over my shoulders. Thus situated, I was able to get his shaft still deeper into my gullet, and he growled his approval. Finally, he was starting to let his inner animal out a bit.

I was actually fine with him not pounding at my mouth: if you want to masturbate, use a fleshlight, not my face. When I'm sucking cock, I prefer to be in control. Ian either was too timid to try anything rougher, or too polite; either way suited me fine. Never once did he wince with the pain of too much teeth, but several times he learned how their gentle, deliberate touch can make it all the better. The ridge at the back of his glans seemed particularly sensitive, and I spent a lot of time running my upper lip to and fro over it, then attending it with my tongue, before taking him entirely within me again. Each time I went through that cycle, it elicited another gasp.

He spread his legs wide, feet in the air, one hand thrown over his face while the other grasped his pubis at the base of his eager cock. I knew he was nearing his climax. This would be the moment when I was unexpectedly shove my tongue or finger up his butt, causing a mind-blowing orgasm and an undeniable need for my cock in his tight young ass. I checked myself: this was a real boy wrapping his legs around my head, because he trusted me to suck his cock like a champ and with discretion. To do anything more would be to violate that trust.

I pulled off to catch my breath and regain control.

"Fuck," he said. "Please don't stop."

That revved me up. Swatting his hand aside, I grabbed him firmly in my own and took him like Tina Turner takes a microphone. I bobbed furiously, stroking at the same time, all while paying attention to Ian's body language. His eyes remained closed, his hands clenched the sheet beneath him, and he again had his legs upon my shoulders, encouraging my head to go down and stay there. He wanted to crawl inside me. His abs were tight, his nipples hard, there were goosebumps forming on his legs and his balls were turning into a walnut. He busted that nut with a loud cry, no longer caring who might hear, and I made sure he was well lodged in my throat to send his sperm straight home. His entire body jerked with each spurt, making it clear how much he was enjoying this orgasm.

With a shudder and a moan, Ian squeezed the last drops out and down my throat. "Fuck," he said breathlessly. "Fuck," he repeated.

I gave him one last milking to make sure he wouldn't leave any telltale stains when he dressed, released his penis from my mouth. It was still hard, but perceptibly smaller than only moments before.

"If that's what birthdays are supposed to feel like, you seriously owe me for the last fifteen," he said.

I just smiled.

Anything Once

Jackson DuPoint

*I*ll be the first to say it. Not the bar type. Usually, if I'm going to drink, I'll do it on my sweet own time in the middle of my living room. No twinks, that you're twice the size of, to sneer at you. No chubby chasers, no baby face chasers, and no bears you're not hairy enough for.

Of course, if you want to meet other queers, you have to swing over to the single, solitary gay bar in town. Or you trek up to Portland, an hour away, and hope you don't look too much like a deer in headlights. Either way, it's leaving the house.

There's Grindr, Surge, sure. But I gave up on those after my thirtieth faceless profile demanded dick pics from little old me.

But somewhere, here I am. I'm sitting at the end of the bar. My buddy's off cruising a table full of bears. Good old Pete. Drags me to the joint for my birthday and jots off and hunts for strange after his third drink. Least he bought my drinks.

I'm sipping on a watermelon vodka. Not the manliest drink, I'll be the first to admit. I'd say I'm doing what I can to defy gender stereotypes but I don't like beer.

There's a drag queen on stage lip-synching to some Cher song that I don't recognize. He's got blood red rouge splayed out across his face, cutting from his cheekbone to his ears. The wig is a bargain mart salvage—stark white with loose curls poking out as if they're trying to run off to Canada. He's wearing a dress that's the same color as his rouge, a Jessica Rabbit-style lounge piece with quarter sized sequins. But he's the best dressed out of any of the other queens and kings who've performed here tonight, which is really saying something. Sundays are drag nights at the bar. Not a drag guy myself but Pete's all for it. And, hey, I wasn't going to turn down a free drink.

About half a dozen guys and girls, half of them straight and together, are sitting around the bar's interior. There's a straight couple noodling together in a booth by the stage and I want to yell at them to get a room. A couple gay guys are nodding along to the Cher song. I'm one of the few guys sitting at the bar, though the other guys at the bar are almost all with someone. Pete's back in the pool room with the bears, who have a game going. I assume he's doing well. He hasn't given me status reports so they must be paying attention to him.

There's a rainbow flag hanging up in the corner right above me. A University of Oregon Ducks game is on the TV. I can't recognize who they're playing against but they seem to be winning. The bartender's absorbed by the game, though. He's cute but he's got a boyfriend. I asked.

I drain down my watermelon vodka and try to get the bartender's attention. He isn't hearing me.

"Hey? Sir?" I wave an arm. Nope. The game's got him now. It's like I'm a ghost.

"Hey!" I call one last time. And then I just suck down the minuscule amount left in my glass.

The Cher song finishes and the drag queen in the red dress steps off the stage to mingle with the crowd. The DJ, a middle-aged guy who squints at a Dell laptop to switch the songs, calls for another drag queen to take the stage. This drag queen's stuck in a cheap white dress that's frayed on the ends. Jet black hair in a wig that looks so stiff, it's practically plastic, hangs down to his flat chest and he's got purple and black eye makeup that was applied with a shaking hand. It's like Elvira on a budget. This queen doesn't lip synch. He sings along to an Evanescence song and boy, do I wish he had lip-synched. He's so off-key, he's invented a whole new one.

"Sir!" A hand reaches over the bar to tap on the bartender's shoulder. "Kid down there wants a drink."

The bartender comes over to me, shaking his head. He's disoriented but he takes my order, another watermelon vodka. He pours it and he's turned his attention back to the Ducks game almost as soon as he's given me the drink.

"Well, hey, thanks—" I search for my savior along the bar. And I settle upon him at the opposite end.

He's not half bad looking. Kind of cute, actually. He's got this hooked Romanesque nose and shaggy brown hair he keeps tucked behind his ear. The guy rubs his strong, slightly cleft jaw. He reminds me a little of Paul Rudd. He's wearing a plaid shirt over a plain black T-shirt and he has a spiral notebook and a tall beer set in front of him. He nods back.

The drag queen's breaking into the song's refrain. "Briiiiiiiiiing me to liiiiiiiiiife!" My cue to get the hell out so I don't have to hear him navigate the key changes. I get up to leave.

"Yeah, you have the right idea," calls the guy.

He follows me out to the smoking patio. I pass through the pool room. Pete's making out with a bear old enough to be my grandfather, with a Santa Claus-style beard. His type, I don't judge.

I'm assaulted by a wave of nicotine and fruit scented vape haze. But the drag queen's song is muffled to a manageable level.

"Jesus," mutters the guy from the bar. He wipes off his forehead with the corner of his plaid shirt. He's got his notebook under one arm. And as he moves to lean against the wall, he yanks a box-shaped contraption out of his pocket. "They gotta put the poor queen out of her misery."

"No kidding." I try to block out what remains of the sound.

He holds the box up to his lips and inhales. Then, he holds it out to me. "Want some? It's Sativa."

He's speaking my language. "You sure?" I want to take it but is it courtesy? I briefly wonder if he's laced it with something but he's already taken another hit. The vapor he breathes out is only vaguely scented with weed. Otherwise, he fits in well with the other vapors in the screened smoking lounge. There's five other guys out here and a single lesbian, all puffing away on their smoking tool of choice. He's the only one with weed.

"Yeah I'm sure," he says. "I'm not just asking cause I like the sound of my voice." His voice is on the high side but it's not reedy. And yet there's a weary element to it.

"Well, sure, I guess." I take it and suck at it. But I get nothing.

"No, you gotta press the button down. Heat the herb up." He gestures to the side of the box.

"Oh." I do as he says and I get a generous blast of vapor in my mouth. I blow it out. I'm a grown man but I still like to imagine I'm a dragon whenever I take a puff of weed. "Well, uh, thanks."

"Mark," he says. He holds out his hand.

"Brody," I return.

"You looked lonely."

"Came with a friend. Just wanted to rest," I say.

"Let me guess. Friend ditched."

"Nah, he's here. Just more social than me."

"Ah." Mark sat down on one of the lounge chairs. He adjusted his posture to spread out his legs and he put his hand behind his head. "You're not anti-social."

"Guess not."

"What you here for?"

"Funny enough, my birthday."

He raises a brow. There's a slight smile curling on Mark's lips. "Well, ah, happy birthday then. Take another puff. On me."

I do. It's good stuff. I already have a nice buzz building up. Though it could be the drinks kicking in. I take another sip of my watermelon vodka. "Yeah, my friend wanted to take me out for drinks. Not usually a bar guy."

"Me neither. I'm doing research."

"For what?"

He pulls out his notebook. "Little article I'm working on."

"You're a reporter?"

"Blogger." He scoffs as if I should've already known that. "Never been to this bar. Don't think I'll be coming back, honestly."

"So what's it about? The, erm, article?"

"Salem's queer scene. I'm pitching an article to one of the local rags on what there is to do and see around here for us queers."

"My advice?" I sit down next to him. "Go up to Portland."

"Looking like it." He sighs. "Some article, eh?"

The drag queen has finally finished butchering the Evanescence song. We both stand up.

"Here. I'll buy you a birthday drink too, how about that?"

"Hey, man, you really don't have to—I already—"

"I need to drink away my memory of that song. You do too," says Mark. And he smiles, wolfishly.

I relent and let him buy the drink. I order something cheap. He goes for another beer.

So far, no new drag queens have taken the stage. The DJ loops Madonna and Cher songs.

"You know, you are cute," says Mark. He swallows down a swig of beer.

"Yeah, that's the beer talking."

"No, really. Got that young Cary Grant thing going."

He's drunk, I'm sure of it. But I shrug it off. "Whatever you say, man." If Cary Grant ate his costars, sure. Then maybe I'd see the resemblance.

"God, you're hard on yourself." He punches me in the arm. It's a light punch that brushes against my skin. "You single?"

"Well, yeah." The pot's getting to me. Or the drink. I have a feeling I know where he's going with this. And I'm caught in the headlights. It's not like I've never been asked out before. It's just not often that it's in person. "You?"

"I have a wife."

"Oh."

He chokes back a sip of beer, laughing. His face is red and flush. "I'm kidding. No worries. Unmarried. Unattached." Mark recovers. "Brody, my friend, I'm shocked. You seem like a decent enough guy."

"You don't even know me."

He shrugs one shoulder. "I'm a pretty good judge of character. Or at least I like to think I am."

And I know when a guy's just trying to get a lay. But I didn't say it. "Are you now?"

"That friend of yours even know you're over here?"

I poke my head around the corner. There's Pete, still hanging around with Santa Claus. "Well, like I said. He's the social one."

Another drag queen takes the stage. It's the Evanescence queen and he seems especially tipsy, the microphone shaking around in his hand.

"Come on," says Mark. He leaps away from the counter. "Let's get the fuck out of here."

"Where are you going?"

"My place. You coming?"

"Wait. What?"

"You heard me." And he heads for the door.

I stand in the middle of the bar. My jaw's slack. The microphone screeches with feedback. The song's about to start.

"If I was you," mutters the bartender. "I'd follow him."

I follow the bartender's advice.

We're driving down Lancaster. It's Sunday and Salem's done for the night. Nothing we pass is open, save for a couple bars and a single McDonalds. And it's hardly midnight.

"I always figure," says Mark. "That you have to be a little spontaneous. At least once in a while. When nothing's going on in your neck of the woods, anyway."

"Like how spontaneous? We talking about, like, random road trips to Alaska spontaneous or trying the new Chinese place across the street?"

"Well, hey, whatever you're cool with." He takes another hit off the vape, blowing the weed-tinged vapor into his Jetta's interior. "You define it how you will."

"Yeah, you're fucking baked," I say.

"Of course," he says. "Usually how I operate."

We trade small talk as we roll down the street. The streets, like the rest of the town, are almost deserted. A homeless man ambles down the intersection with a cart piled high with pet food. My head's spinning and it's not from anything I've consumed since leaving the bar. I take another couple of hits off of the vaporizer.

I text Pete. He won't respond until half past four but at least he won't worry about leaving his charge alone in the middle of the bar.

"But anyway, I'm proud of you," says Mark. He turns down a side street, into an apartment complex.

"For *what*?"

"I dunno. Letting your hair down just a little. I get the feeling you don't do it that often."

"Guess you'd be right." And he was. I'm not a party guy. Beyond Dungeons and Dragons with my old college friends, but who's counting? I was a teetotaler in college, which I'd only just graduated from a couple years ago. When I had to write about notable life events for college application essays, I used extensively edited excerpts from my half-orc barbarian's backstory. I wish I was kidding.

"Well, we're here." We pull into a parking lot right in front of a weathered apartment building. He slips out of the front seat, like a cat, and comes around to the passenger side to wait for me.

His apartment is three stories up and by the time we clamber up to his door, I'm out of breath and resting my hands on my knees.

"Well, welcome to Chez Mark." He pushes the door open, which briefly sticks.

The apartment is a one-room, with a futon slapped down in the far corner of the room. There's a kitchenette but otherwise, the only other room is a bathroom off next to the futon. Still, despite its size, it's fairly neat. He's got hundreds of books alphabetized on a wall-length IKEA shelf. There's little clutter, beyond all of the knickknacks and pot paraphernalia organized along various floating shelves and on top of the bookshelf. An iMac is set up on the kitchen counter. There doesn't seem to be any sign of a spouse around. I find myself sighing with relief. No awkward encounters with a betrayed wife, hopefully.

"Not much," says Mark. "But it's home."

"Hey, it's fine to me." I can only think about how blissful it's gotta be to have an apartment to himself. My roommates, Pete being one of them, aren't dicks. But they're not the quiet types.

He doesn't usher me to the futon. Instead, he gets a bong together and pops a fat and intact nugget of weed he retrieves from a Mason jar labeled "Pink Lemonade" in the bowl. He motions me over to the sofa, a neglected thing covered in old blankets, across from the kitchenette.

"So why all this?" I take the bong when he offers it and I heat up the nugget with a cigarette lighter. I nearly burn my thumb trying to get a hit but, soon, smoke clouds in the chamber and I'm off to a good start. The smoke cuts at the inside of my throat but it's strong stuff and I hold it in for a few moments before exhaling. I still cough as I exhale.

"You're clearly not the bar type," says Mark. "Figured this was more your scene."

I'm still coughing. If it's off-putting, he doesn't pay it any mind.

"And it's not just because you want in my pants."

He takes two hits without even coughing, choking down a laugh. "In all honesty, my friend, it wouldn't be a bad way to end tonight."

And that's the moment he leans in, his lips meeting mine.

I'll never know if it was just the watermelon vodkas talking but in that moment, it's the most natural thing that could have happened.

My mouth is pressing back against his. His stubble's rubbing up against my chin, his tongue hunts for mine. Mark's lips are soft and he's the best thing I've ever tasted in that moment.

He pulls back just as my pants tighten around my growing bulge. "That okay?" He's rubbing at the back of his neck. The bong has been set down and it's forgotten.

"More than okay," I answer back. And he comes right back in for more.

His weight sinks into mine, arms wrapping around my chest. And when he straddles my lap with his thighs hugging my hips, he sidles back when his crotch meets my bulge. "I can see that," he says.

He's got a bulge of his own but he keeps it a centimeter or two away from me, not letting it come into direct contact, though the rest of his body melts into mine.

His hair, his scent, the weed—I take it all in.

Mark breaks away from my mouth, pulling up my shirt. His mouth trails down my chest and I have to force myself to not flip about my belly fat. He's planting kissing and tapping at my bare skin with his tongue. I push into him, my hands grasping the back of his head and keeping him anchored to me.

He unzips my jeans and my cock springs out of my boxers. His mouth curls around my shaft, his tongue teases my head. I'm putty under his craftsmanship. He's sucking hard and moving his mouth up and down my cock. And I'm doing what I can not to come as soon as he's on me.

I run my fingers through his hair, letting each strand fall through my fingers. And he sucks harder, my body's electric.

He comes up for air and meets my lips again. My cock's stiff now and I'm craving release. But he doesn't immediately return to sucking. He kneels down to caress and lick my thighs, yanking my boxers and jeans down to my ankles as he settles on the floor in front of me.

"Wait." I move to take his shirt off but he brushes my hands away. "I want to return the favor."

"Just relax, birthday boy." And he returns to sucking my cock without any pomp or circumstance.

But I'm going soft, even as he sucks harder and takes me in deeper. "There's something wrong."

He meets my gaze, swiping saliva from the corner of his lips. "I knew this was stupid."

"I just want you to enjoy yourself too, that's all."

Instead of returning to finish the blowjob, he takes another hit off the bong. He does not offer it to me. He's sitting next to my legs, crouched on the floor, and turned away from me. "Sorry. I just get...edgy."

"Should I leave?"

"No, you can stay. It's cool. I just need a moment." And he stalks off to the bathroom, leaving me alone on his couch.

And that would be my luck. Hooking up and not even getting to finish. Just as I go to text Pete and beg for a ride back to my place, Mark returns from the bathroom. He's taken off his plaid shirt and he strides back over in his black t-shirt. It highlights his biceps and it's clear he lifts.

The storm that was brewing seems to have passed. He's calm and he plops back on the couch next to me.

I try to kiss him. He pushes me back. "Hey, now," he says. "Let it be clear. You're cute. You don't think it but you're not a bad guy. Loads of guys—they'd kill for a little bear cub like you. Got a good thing going."

"But—" I take the bong when he hands it to me. "There's a catch, isn't it?"

"You're a lot like me, honest. Acting like you have a deal breaker on board."

"What are you talking about?"

"Well, I have one myself."

"Come on," I say. "You're fine. Nothing wrong with you." And it's then that it hits me. He's married. Or he's got a girlfriend who, at any moment, will come storming into the apartment and chase me out with a broom.

"I...haven't been exactly forthcoming about myself."

Here we go. The girlfriend.

"I've got a weird fucking body."

"Oh jeez, you think that's a big deal? Look at me!"

"No. You don't get it." He says it through his teeth. "It was stupid of me to do this."

"How bad can it honestly be?"

And he moves to unbuckle his belt. "You take these off, you're not going to see a cock. At least not in the conventional sense." His voice betrays his attempt at being casual.

I don't say anything more. My attention is rapt. His hands are shaking as he fumbles with the belt and the top button of his jeans. I want to go help him. He seems so vulnerable now and as he yanks down his jeans, it's impossible not to notice the wince he gives as he grasps the top of his briefs. There is a bulge in his briefs—the outline of a dick—but it hangs at an odd angle.

He reaches in the front of his briefs and takes the bulge out. It's a peach-colored mold of a dick, with a loopy shaft that hugs a pair of far too-round balls. This he sets on the kitchen counter as he walks over to the couch. His crotch is now flat and formless, with curls of hair poking out over the waistband.

I'm catching his meaning now. And I say nothing, just take it all in, as he moves to finally slip off his briefs.

His junk's exposed. A light patch of dark hair swarms up from between his legs, meeting up with a long happy trail. And right between his legs is a small pink nub poking out from underneath his pubic hair, a fat little mound of flesh. It's his cock—or clit, I'm not sure what to call it—and my eyes lock onto it.

"Well, that's it," says Mark. He chuckles but it's not particularly convincing.

"So you're—"

"Trans?" He sighs. "Yeah. No surgeries. Except for up here." And he rolls off his shirt. Two rose-colored scars roll underneath his pecs.

He's just as naked as I am and I take him all in. He's got the beginnings of abs forming over his chest. And he's far hairier than I am. If he grew out his beard, he would give the bears a run for their money. I try not to stare at his chest scars or his junk. It's not the first time I've seen a trans man. Once, I stumbled upon a Buck Angel porno years ago. I wasn't sure what to think. And I guess I don't know what to think right now as Mark stands before me.

He sits down back next to me. "I dunno. I worry about telling people all the time. And if you're not cool with it..."

"Nah, it's." I stumble over my words. "Just unexpected."

The wolfish grin returns. He's almost flushing.

"Shit, man, I thought you were married."

"No, not lucky enough for that yet," he says. He laughs.

We take more hits off the bong.

"I've just never..." I gesture to his junk. "Been with anyone..."

"You can say it. You've never fucked a trans guy." He breathes out a puff of smoke through his nostrils. "You think most of the guys I've hooked with are well versed in that department? I beg to differ. Course, usually, most of the time, I never take off my pants."

"Well, why not? You just...hate your body or what?"

"Not so much me." He shrugged. "I don't always get guys who are really...receptive."

"Oh."

"Yeah." He breathes his next puff out slowly. "So, erm. Not to be blunt but you want to—" He gestures to the futon but I get the hint.

"I guess I'll try anything once," I say. And I come onto him, going for his lips.

And maybe it's just the weed but in that moment, he's the best thing I've ever tasted and the best thing I ever will. My hands explore his body, flowing along each contour and groove. He's pushing himself into me and he's stroking my shaft. It doesn't take me long to roar to life again and my cock tenses up against his crotch. His own nub of a cock tenses up, stiffening under my touch. The wetness that collects underneath his cock, flowing from his front hole, is alien but it's warm and silken. Everything between his legs is swollen with heat and lust and I rub the palm of my hand against his little cock and his hole.

He moans, humping my hand. His back curls back and he kisses me back forcibly.

I bring my cock to rub against his, pleasuring him with my head. He's straddling my lap now and he spreads his junk open to help it curl around my shaft, taking me in close.

I push him back onto the couch and pull his legs apart. "Need to return the favor," I tell him. His junk is strange, foreign. But it's a good kind of strange. I bury my mouth between his legs, flicking his cock with my tongue.

"Jesus," he moans. He thrusts his hips towards my mouth. "*Jesus fucking Christ.*"

My lips curl around his cock and I suck, whipping the head of his little cock with the tip of my tongue. He's going crazy now, hardening up even more and moaning louder. His thighs squeeze the side of my temples and he's pulling me in deeper.

I pull away just as I'm sensing he's about to overload with ecstasy. And he knows my next move. He leads me to the futon and digs a condom out of his nightstand. I fumble with it, nearly dropping it several times before I finally secure it over me. I'm not saying it's been a long time since I've fucked a guy but usually, I'm not the one on top when it does happen. As he directs me to lie on my back, he's guiding my shaft between his legs as he sinks into my lap. And then, he takes me inside his foreign hole. Heated walls, soft and yet tense all the same, pulse and squeeze around me. He's guiding my movements with the rhythm of his body, grinding against my crotch. His little cock tenses and swells against my gut. In this moment, we're one person.

I have to bite the inside of my cheek to stop myself from coming too fast. And it won't take much for him to come either. He's grinding harder and harder with each thrust I give, squeezing my shaft with his entrance tighter and tighter. With how fast and hard we're going, I'm doing what I can to keep the condom from slipping off.

And just when I'm about to release and explode inside him, he leaps off of my lap.

"How about I take a turn?" He fishes out a dildo from the nightstand. But it's unlike any dildo I've seen before. It's flesh colored and realistically painted, with a rose colored head over a peach shaft. A thick bulb protrudes from the opposite end. "My prosthetic. You get to help break him in."

I'm dying for the release. I'm tense and throbbing painfully. So I nod as he inserts the bulb into his front entrance.

I stroke and pull at the shaft of his prosthetic. His own cock rubs against the base of the prosthetic and he's writhing with pleasure as I manipulate the prosthetic harder and faster.

He stops me and pushes me onto my hands and knees. The lube's cold as he squeezes it out of a bottle from the nightstand drawer but he applies it to my ass with careful strokes.

He inserts one finger after the other, stretching me out and relaxing me enough to thrust inside. When he finds my prostate and begins to massage it, pressure builds in my shaft.

As he gets up to three fingers fitting inside me without pain, he pulls his hand out and pushes the prosthetic inside.

His shaft is hard and stiff and he manipulates himself and my position to give him the best access to my prostate. And once I moan and my knees begin to shake, he thrusts. The thrusts start out gentle and deep as if he's finding his footing.

"You're doing good," I tell him. But it's hard to speak when I've got a cock up my ass. "Deeper. You can do it."

And he relents. He pushes in deeper, his crotch buried against me as he presses and pulses. I can feel his own nub stiffen and thump as he works the prosthetic. I grasp his bedsheets under my palms, anchoring myself. We moan in unison as he thrusts faster and harder. My cock is stiff and wild and I'm rubbing my own shaft as he lays kisses and licks up and down my spine while he works.

"Aw shit," he says.

And I fear the worst for a moment. His body pushes away from my own. The prosthetic is still inside me, but he kneels away.

"It's supposed to be strapless," he says. "But I guess that wasn't enough to keep it in."

"Well, fuck that. Come here."

I guide him this time as he sets the prosthetic aside and turns around to straddle my chest. He lies on me, scooting so he's on all fours and my neck is between his thighs. And though he's slightly shorter than me, he's still able to curl his lips around my cock.

I lick his nub and hole, grabbing his hips to pull him in. And he moves his mouth up and down my shaft, taking me in. I try to hold back but it's not long before I explode in his mouth. And as I come, he grinds against my tongue. As he gasps for breath, I penetrate him with my tongue, feeling his walls around with the tip. And it's then, as I move in and out, flipping a hand around to rub his cock as I work, that he comes, groaning with release.

We gasp for breath as he rolls off me and lies beside me on the futon. We're flush with heat and perspiration.

"Have to say," he says, going for the bong. "You're not half bad."

"Did pretty well yourself," I answer, taking a hit when he offers it to me.

And we lie together for some time, remaining silent. His heart's beating rapidly in his chest. Everything's kicking in now and the colors in his room seem somehow more vibrant, the feeling of his body next to mine even stronger than it was before.

I hold him close. He's so quiet that, at first, I assume he's fallen asleep but he speaks after a while. "You have to give yourself more credit," he says.

"And—and you too. Don't hide from guys, okay? You'll find guys who aren't gonna mind. I mean, I really didn't."

He grins. "Well, you're probably right."

"We ever going to do this again?'

He moves to throw his clothes back on, slipping on his briefs and jeans. He sits back on the edge of the futon, shirtless. And to my question, he responds with a shrug. "You never know. Guess we'll see what happens."

*W*e trade numbers before he drives me home. And when we finally get back to my apartment, I watch him when he drives away.

"So, good time?' Pete's watching Netflix on his phone when I pass through the living room.

"You didn't go home with anyone?" I sit down on the couch next to him.

"Nah, man," says Pete. "Guy I was gonna go with had a wife. She was gonna join in. Not my thing."

"Nah, wouldn't be."

"Sorry I left you. Dick move."

I shrug. "Worked out in the end." And when I finally stumble to my room, I'm practically skipping like an idiot.

I empty my pockets before throwing my jeans off and it's then that I feel it. I fish out a half-dollar sized nugget of weed in a Zip-loc bag. A note's been attached. I open and read it out loud.

Happy birthday. Let your hair down once in a while.—M.

I set the weed in my pipe and puff away, unable to kill the stupid grin on my face.

When Needs Befall

Atom Yang

*J*ohn stood in the alley with the restaurant's kitchen door behind him. The stink of garbage—reminiscent of the rotten taste of *kombucha* he had tried once in a health food store—wafted past him, mixed with the smell of urine and sewage. The backs of restaurants were rarely as glamorous as their fronts, not that his restaurant could be considered glamorous by any of the orange chicken and sweet-and-sour pork ordering regulars he served.

He glanced down at his scarred forearms crossed in front of his apron, and they shone with the grease of a busy day. So many egg rolls and fried wontons. It was a culinary hell that no Food Network show would ever feature—but then again, they didn't seem to feature hardly any Asian chefs despite the predominance of Asian food in global cuisine.

He raked a hand through his thick hair and it stayed where he had combed it. He had always wished for manageable hair like the American guys at school had, whose manes grew away from their faces instead of toward them. John had suffered through the inevitable and unenviable bowl haircut his pragmatic and frugal mother gave him during his formative years, and fumed in his room with the fury of a samurai whose family had been murdered when he picked up the nickname "Dickhead" because any complaint he might have voiced would have been seen as ingratitude—replete with comparisons about how his hair reflected his character: unruly, stubborn, and disobedient.

John glanced at the moon and inhaled. Despite the noxious perfume of the alleyway with its trash bins, the crisp night air cooled his lungs, a contrast from the fire and smoke of the kitchen. He ran his fingers through his hair again and rubbed his thumb and fingers together, feeling the oil from the day's cooking. Perhaps without it weighing his hair down, he would have resembled the abused end of an old toothbrush, its bristles splayed by aggression against plaque.

He planned on following the wasteful directions on the shampoo bottle tonight. Lather. Rinse. Repeat. Maybe repeat again after that if he felt it necessary. He could save himself a lot of trouble if he'd just wear a shower cap while he stir-fried like his mother suggested, but after the bowl haircut of his adolescence, a shower cap would have cremated whatever was left of his self-esteem.

John leaned against the metal grate of the kitchen door. Everybody had gone home as usual while he had prepped for tomorrow. It was just him and that uncanny, ghost town feeling a restaurant has when it's closed.

He reached into his back pocket and pulled out a tin that had once carried his grandmother's favorite hard candies. They were fruit-flavored and every time he visited her, she'd give him one. He loved all the flavors equally and delighted in the dusty coat of sugar that dissolved in the drool and excitement of childhood. One time, when she had given him the last candy, she offered him the tin, too, and he had kept it all these years, opening it to smell its fragrance whenever he missed his grandmother.

These days, he stored a joint or two and strike-anywhere matches in it. They became fruit scented as well, although this transference grew weaker over time. One day, he knew, it would only smell of pot, and he had accepted that this would be the scent of comfort. An adult clung to different things than a kid.

John's greasy fingers slipped a few times before he pried open the tin, and once the lid clicked past the locking indentation where the paint had been scuffed off, he moved with the care of his Jewish friends when they read from the *Torah* for their bar mitzvahs. The hinge of the lid squeaked as he repositioned the tin in his palm and brought it up to his nose. Fading nostalgia mingled with an herbaceous promise.

He looked up and down the alley for signs of complex life and finding none, he sparked the doobie, closed his eyes, and sucked in a lungful that evicted the night air he had taken in previously, replacing it with spicy smoke that slunk into the very architecture of his body.

"You mind?"

John coughed the type of cough that might leave him with a sore throat the next morning. Smoke billowed from his mouth and he croaked, "What the fuck...?"

The security lamp high above them on the opposite wall shadowed the face of the man standing in front of him. "Sorry, I didn't mean to scare you."

John shaded his watering eyes and waved the smoke away. "Hey, if you want some food," he rasped, "I can fix you something quick, but you have to stay out here."

The man moved so John could see him without the light haloing him from behind. He wore an eyepatch, not the kind from a clinic, but black and tailored to the hollow between his brow and cheek like a pirate's. John realized there and then that he had always wanted to see someone wearing an eyepatch outside of a cartoon or movie or sight-saving operation, and at the same time, that he was a dick for wanting such a shitty thing since someone had to lose an eye for him to get his wish.

"Naw, I don't need any food." The man smiled, and his teeth were as pale as a sidewalk. "I just followed my nose. Wondering if you wouldn't mind sharing some." He gestured at John's fatty.

John examined his hand as if he didn't know his fingers pinched a wizard between them. He glanced back at the man—gray-bearded and broad-shouldered, lean but not gaunt, and built in a way that suggested more acquaintance with a shovel and a trench than a dumbbell and a gym—his larger figure might have intimidated John, yet the man remained a respectful distance away and made no move to pressure him into compliance. If he had worn a wool cap, he would have held it in his large hands now and maybe wrung it with the humility of a Great Depression hobo.

What if he has hepatitis or something?

A huge raven landed on a nearby trash bin, the sound of its wings no more distinct than scraps of paper blowing down the alley. Its claws tapped lightly on the rubber lid and then it hopped toward them before bellowing an accusatory caw. It then flew away, its darkness blending in with the darkness of the night.

"I don't have any diseases if you're worried," the man said, "and I give you my word I will not Bogart."

John blushed. "I wasn't worried." He eyed the man and decided that, for being in the hospitality business, he had not been hospitable to someone who wanted no more than a toke, and this was not how he wanted to see himself. "Here."

The man approached without hurry and plucked the smoldering J from John's outstretched hand, careful not to touch him in the transfer, and lingered a moment before bringing the Scooby Snack to his chest and repositioning it within the shelter of his curved fingers and palm, a fire within a cave. He closed his eyes and sniffed the fractal smoke. "Thank you."

"No problem, buddy."

John watched him take a drag, the lit end racing fiercely toward the man's lips. His nails were clean and evenly cut, without the usual grime and lack of grooming John noticed on the people he found scavenging the city. The stranger's construction worker boots were sturdy and well-worn, creased with time and labor; the neatly tied laces still had their plastic tips. Nothing about him appeared frayed or forgotten. He only had the dust of miles on him.

The man handed the tokémon back to John, who blazed until he burned his fingers. He considered the roach before dropping it to his feet and then grinding it out for good measure; since legalization in his state, he could afford to toss this bit instead of engineering a contraption to squeeze the vestiges of THC out of each precious speck of bud. John held his breath and they stared at each other with chests puffed like roosters in a cockfight before the stranger issued curling clouds into the cold air. It seemed to take forever for him to empty his lungs.

John followed suit, venting from the corner of his mouth the way he had spied his uncles and their friends doing as they chain-smoked cigarettes while playing mahjong late at night, their eyes squinting with the virility of cowboys dueling under a blazing sun.

"You sure you don't want anything to eat?"

"Well, if you're offering," the man answered with a chuckle and shy smile. "I wouldn't mind a bite if it's no bother."

Mary Jane sang in John's body, tingling his fingertips and toes, filling him from his extremities to his center with a magical stuffing that would bring his rag doll self to life. Between his legs, his prostate swelled and poached like an egg from the bamba simmering in his blood. "Come in, I'll fix you something. It'll be my pleasure and privilege."

John opened the metal security door and ushered the man inside, inhaling deeply as the tall stranger walked past him. He smelled woodsy and leathery, a grandfather's favorite jacket spiced with age and smoke and sweat. John laid a hand lightly on the man's back, between the shoulder blades, to welcome him into his kitchen, and for a moment, he felt insignificant and in the presence of a mountain that even the sky could not conquer.

And this made John hard.

He trailed behind and the cheap door closer up top, which kept the door from slamming and banging each time someone exited or entered, whined as the piston pushed the air out of it. "It'll just take a sec," John said.

"I'm in no hurry."

John took that as honest permission to chill and strolled around the man to turn on the fan under the range hood. He lit the stove, setting a heavy wok black with years of seasoning onto a ring of blue flames. He ambled to the walk-in refrigerator and came back with an armload of cold rice, mixed vegetables, a bit of barbecue pork, and a couple of eggs.

"Who's this?" The stranger pointed at an illustration of a beard-ed man in ancient Chinese garb with children playing at his feet taped to the wall near the range. Laid out before the image were two electric candles—not the battery-powered, realistic kind made with wax that sold in high-end furniture stores, but two red plastic tubes decorated with gold dragons and topped with crimson bulbs that flickered. Between the candles was a small soup bowl of ash-covered rice grains with the remainder of three joss sticks stuck into them, and in front of this was a plate of three tangerines.

"He's *Zao Shen*, the Kitchen God, also known as *Zao Jun*, the Stove Master." John set his ingredients down and removed the lids to the peanut oil and soy sauce next to the wok which had be-gun smoking. "Every year, he reports to the Emperor of Heaven about the family he watches over, who then metes out punish-ments or rewards."

The stranger considered the altar. "The Romans had *Lares*."

"Household gods, right? All these deities get blended and mixed up over time as people move around and beliefs change. It's how they stay immortal." John had loved mythology as a kid. He would have majored in religious studies had he been able to go to college. His mother needed him too much.

"The Catholics built their churches on top of sacred pagan sites. Made it easier to convert people from worshiping the Earth Mother into adoring the Virgin Mary. Funny how minor gods become major, and major gods become minor."

John tilted his head in deference. "You're very knowledgeable." He had never had a conversation about this topic in this kitchen, and now he was having it with some dude off the street while they were both stoned. A distant part of him, like a favorite marble that's fallen irretrievably down a sink, twinkled up, just out of reach.

"I'm familiar." The man glanced at John and looked away. "When you've hung around as long as I have, you learn things."

John poured oil into the wok and swirled it quickly to coat the sides before sliding in chopped green onion circles that popped happily. A roar of sizzling applause followed when John used the spatula to tumble in the cubed, scarlet meat. He stirred rapidly.

"Anyway, the Kitchen God is sort of a patron saint like the Lares. He watches over people." John looked up to see the stranger observing him cook, and he tossed in the peas and diced carrots, mixing everything together. He raised his voice above the fan and sounds of cooking. "Except he's like *Elf on a Shelf*, too, with reporting to the Big Guy around Christmastime about who's naughty or nice."

The stranger glanced up from the wok and John winked at him before dumping in the rice. It was cold and the clumps broke apart easily under his ministrations, which muffled the sizzling.

"There's another tradition, though, and that's smearing honey on his lips." John dribbled soy sauce over everything and folded it in, again and again, darkening the fried rice. "It either ensures he sweet talks to the Emperor or his mouth is too sticky to spill any beans." John reached for the two eggs, a sheen of moisture over their cool shells registering in his dry palms. He cracked them perfectly on each side of the wok, single-handedly at the same time, to show off. "It's weird when you think about how easy it is to curry favor with deities. Burn a little something fragrant, give 'em some fruit, maybe a shot of whiskey, or sacrifice a virgin if you want some awesome crops, and they're happy to oblige." The whites and yolks rolled into the rice, leaving white trails on the heated iron. John stabbed them with his spatula and blended them into the rice.

"It doesn't take much, does it? Where are your bowls?"

"Over there." John bobbed his head and stuck out his lower lip to emphasize the direction. "Chopsticks are below. Do you need a fork?"

"I think I can manage."

He added salt to taste and tossed the fried rice several times into the air before mounding the bowls ridiculously high. "In Chinese, we say *man man chr*. It essentially means, 'take your time eating.'"

The stranger smiled. "People here say 'dig in,' right? As if speed made everything better." He pulled up two stools and sat in one of them, his feet perched on the lower ring that stabilized the stool's three legs. Two pairs of chopsticks, slotted inside paper sleeves, rested on his lap.

The man took out his pair and broke them apart with a snap. "I sometimes feel like I should make a wish before I do that." He refrained from rubbing them against each other—which some people did to remove possible splinters that John had never encountered in all his years—and held the utensils expertly, his fingers positioned in a way that was not merely functional, but beautiful. The mundane tools appeared more delicate for being in his large hand, and John wondered where the man had learned to wield chopsticks with such elegance, and who had taken the time to teach him.

"You're talented with those," John said, aiming his chin for clarification. He handed him a bowl of fried rice and the man traded him a pair of chopsticks for it.

"I had to practice, but thank you. You're the first one to notice." He partook in the aroma of his food with the same reverence and intensity as he had blasted the stick outside. When he finally exhaled, John half-expected a veil of smoke to issue from his nostrils to envelop his munchies companion like before. "And thank you for this."

"You might not like it."

"I have no doubt I'll love it."

"Marijuana makes everything taste better, I know."

"Generosity and gratitude make everything taste better, too."

John had forgotten that the man was homeless and that he probably received good, hot food only once a day at a soup kitchen if he were lucky.

Had this man said he was homeless? He had only asked if John would share his weed, he hadn't declared a state of emergency in terms of shelter. Names were confusing—the homeless, hobos, street people, beggars, vagrants, vagabonds, drifters, transients, tramps...what did all the labels mean in the end? His mind raced on a hamster wheel of righteous-bush-infused philosophy and politics and then screeched to a halt as he observed the person eating before him.

The stranger had a blade of a nose, long with a high bridge, and prominent cheekbones covered with a trimmed beard that now had a few grains sticking to it. He was handsome if a little haggard, a tired warrior that had seen things in his day rather than a disillusioned desk jockey eating his weight in uncomfortable feelings.

The man shoveled the fried rice directly from his bowl with his chopsticks, in the Chinese style, and his hunger warmed John's heart. Isn't this why his mother brushed his hair and watched while he ate what she made for him? This was also why he had enjoyed cooking—before he became a cook and became trapped in the kitchen with grease and noise and the latest food trends of *no carbs* or *gluten-free* imposed on his centuries-old recipes and the random but reliable accusations every so often by rowdy customers of serving lost neighborhood pets. The Kitchen God had been his friend all this time, the only one to hear his muttered complaints, fantastic revenge plots, and dreams without offering any irritating advice.

"Oh, crap!" John set down his emptied bowl on a counter, wiped his lips with the back of his hand, and rested his chopsticks next to the bowl rather than on top; his grandmother had gotten on his case for not having manners when he did that, and he never forgot the lesson. "I totally spaced offering you something to drink. You want a beer?"

The man swallowed his final bite and sighed with satisfaction as if he had completed a bucket-list marathon. "That was the best fried rice I've ever had. And I would love a beer."

John returned with two Tsingtaos and popped the caps off them. He handed one to the man and they clinked bottlenecks. "*Ganbei!*"

"*Skål!*"

They chugged, the golden lager flowing down with ease, cold and rejuvenating, maximizing the flavors of their recently finished meal.

"Is that Danish?" John thought of a group of Danes who had eaten at his restaurant and insisted he join in their revelry. They had cried "skål" each time they wanted everyone to shoot aquavit and eventually passed out an hour after closing. John had mercifully sent his wait staff home earlier, thanking them for their patience, but he had not realized that the young man he felt staring at him the whole time had been waiting for this moment to have John to himself. While his friends slept and snored, the two pounded away in a booth in the back using makeshift plastic food wrap condoms and peanut oil as lube until their orgasms were dry, their throats hoarse, their legs shook, and the Dane's friends stirred. John had crossed his heart about visiting the guy in Denmark, but years had passed with no opportunity and never enough funds for him to leave work and travel, and their emails eventually dwindled to annual holiday greetings sprinkled with hope.

Outside the kitchen, another raven, or the same one as before, squawked. Perhaps disturbed by the light pollution and nonstop urban activity, these birds had stayed awake past their normal bedtime. Cities, the larger they got, not only created oddities, they invited them.

"It's an old Viking toast."

"Would you like to make another one?"

The man placed his bottle on the counter, the distinctive clunk echoing the hollowness inside. "I should thank you for your hospitality. It's rare these days."

John got up from his stool and averted his eyes. "Oh, no need to thank me. I guess you have to get going."

"Not yet." The stranger stepped off his stool and sauntered the short distance to John, who remained seated with his knees apart and his own empty bottle held casually at his crotch. The man grasped the bottle and waited for John to let go before taking it and setting it aside. He massaged John's shoulders, releasing an involuntary groan from him.

"You really don't have to thank me. It's cool." Each squeeze of the man's powerful fingers sent shivers down his spine that gathered in the tip of his cock. He swallowed and his eyelids fluttered shut. "Not that I'm going to stop you from doing this."

The man chuckled again, an addictive sound soft as wings flapping toward the earth, feathers shushing and whispering of the air above. "Why don't you take off your shirt?"

John's heart skittered in his chest like minced garlic in hot oil. "I need a shower. I'm coated in sweat and grease."

The man met John's concern with a steady, cyclopean gaze and a single bushy brow raised in question. "Is that why you smell delicious?" That chuckle again, and John's balls shifted inside his jeans as his cock thickened. "Frankly, it might make giving you a back rub easier."

"Don't say I didn't warn you." John hopped off his stool and undid his apron, then took off his shirt, and laid both on the counter beside them. He lifted an arm to sniff his armpit playfully, and before he brought it down again, the man clasped his triceps and stuck his nose into the tender pocket of skin, inhaling deeply and tickling John with breath and beard.

"Yes, you smell delicious. Like jasmine in tea. Lavender in cookies. Ganja in sweat. Something unexpected."

John stared at him. "I stink."

"Not to me you don't."

"Will you take off your shirt, too?"

"Why don't you do it?"

John's cock crouched inside his underwear, an overwound spring threatening to break.

He reached up to the man's collar and undid each button, the stranger's body heat permeating the fabric like the warm spot on a bed after a lover's left. As he opened the shirt, silver and black hair unfurled—animal under the clothing of civilization—a luxurious pelt that reached from gullet to groin. He pushed the shirt edges back, brushing past the nipples that instantly hardened, and shuffled the shirt off the square shoulders, tugging at the wrists where the cuffs caught, and then bringing it all to his face where he inhaled, saturating himself with the man's scent, getting high off it as he drank in the sight of the massive chest that had lain hidden under the unassuming clothes. John shook out the shirt, folded it, and placed it on the counter, on top of his own shirt. He patted it once before letting it go.

"You're very thoughtful."

Heat blossomed on John's face and he touched the shiny, metal band on the man's ropy-veined arm, right below the curve of the brawny shoulder. "Where'd you get that?"

"It was a gift, one of the few things I kept from my old life." John imagined the unspoken part of that sentence was, "before I lost everything." The man stroked the band with a thumb. "It's made of gold."

John's maternal grandparents had a small jewelry store in Hong Kong, and they had given him rings and small amulets decorated with protective Buddhist, Taoist, and Catholic divinities—they weren't picky—for every one of his birthdays until his grandfather died and his grandmother retired from the business and sent cash in red envelopes instead. John had sold the last of his jewelry a few years ago to settle some debts, and the pain of giving them up prevented him from making the callous suggestion that this man do the same so he could—what? Live the life of a domesticated water buffalo with a yoke on its back like him? "The artisanship is stunning. I can see why you still have it."

"Thank you." The stranger bent to John's height and studied his face.

"Yes?"

The man lunged and kissed him, catching John's head and cradling it with his enormous paws.

John's devoured yelp at the stranger's frightening passion gave way to a low moan, the thin collar of restraint on the larger man's wolfish desire exhilarating him. In the back of his mind, he registered the wetness in his shorts as being pre-cum squirted out each time his ass had clenched to this man's expression of hunger for him.

The fried rice had slicked their lips, felt as heavy as lip gloss on a seventh-grade girl John had kissed in a closet on a dare, tasted like pork and egg and rice and soy sauce. John nibbled on the man's lower lip, sucked on it greedily to feel its slipperiness, returned for more and the stranger met him with another desperate kiss that sealed their mouths against each other.

The man's tongue flicked between John's teeth, viper strikes that called for John's tongue to defend its home, to come out and wrestle with it.

John unbuckled the stranger's belt and unbuttoned his jeans. No underwear. A grandfather clock had nothing on the pendulum swinging between the stranger's legs. John squeezed it, and the man grunted into his mouth for a second before resuming his kisses, and then John tugged on the stiff, silky shaft as he guided them to the front of the restaurant.

The man followed, shuffling and smiling with his pants around his ankles. "Hold on a sec." He took off his boots and shucked off his pants, and stood in bare, naked glory except for the eyepatch, armband, and socks.

John wrapped his hand around the man's cock again, reveling in its girth as he would an outstanding specimen of daikon, and led them to a booth reserved for prep work such as folding cloth napkins or breaking the tough ends off string beans. The staff never sat customers back here.

John shoved the rectangular table to the side so that it covered the bench opposite the one he wanted to use, giving the stranger space to spread out if needed, and he anticipated he would. He maneuvered the man to the red vinyl-covered seat where he sat down and raised his gaze to John.

As the man unbuckled John's belt in turn, John toed off his shoes. After the stranger undid his pants, John shoved everything down in one sweeping motion and kicked the discarded clothing aside. His cock bobbed painfully in time with his heart and his balls withdrew inside him.

"You're beautiful."

John observed the swaying spear of his companion. "I think I'm going to write a poem about yours."

The stranger chuckled and this extracted a bead of pre-cum out of John's cock which he did not miss. He reached a long arm between John's legs and cupped his ass, pulling John to his waiting mouth, the force of his hand making John tiptoe forward or fall until the man swallowed him whole and made him cry out with pleasure.

John rocked onto the balls of his feet, gazed half-lidded at the suspended ceiling of the restaurant, not forgetting where he was and would be for the rest of his life, but for the moment, not caring. The man slid up and down his cock, hot and slippery, and John imagined he could fly soon if the man did not stop what he was doing.

"I want you inside me." He continued to pump John's dick but with his hand, moving languidly from the mushroom head to the root.

John landed—his heels touched the ground and he looked down at the stranger, whose eyebrows steepled in earnestness and swollen lips glistened. "I'll be right back."

The man's grip tightened and he stopped moving. "You're safe with me. I give you my word." The man leaned back on one elbow and hooked his large feet around John's hips, rubbing them against his cheeks and nudging him closer.

More pre-cum extruded from John's boner. The stranger sat up again, his abdomen flexing, and he dabbed a calloused finger on the fluid, collecting it like an errant drip of honey. He coated his lips with it and smiled.

John considered the pressure of his nut growing inside him, crowding out other thoughts. He wanted to take the chance—so what if it would be with a one-eyed wanderer with a gold armband and sexy laugh? The man was gorgeous, he wanted John, and life was for the living, however long they remained living.

He spat on his hand and swathed his cock, the saliva mixing with his pre-cum to form an organic lubricant. He spat again, wetting his dick until it shined.

"You don't have to worry about that. Not with me."

"I don't want to hurt you."

"You won't."

The man's cock throbbed like the ticking of a second hand, and John bowed to take it into his mouth, circumnavigating the space between foreskin and head with his tongue, devouring the tang and saltiness while swaddled in a musk that smelled of forests after rains.

John choked with his efforts, involuntary tears gumming his eyes. He wanted all the dick, he wanted to feel it stretch him until there was no space for him to fret about what he was doing or how he would feel about it tomorrow.

Gentle hands lifted his head and John relented, sucking and swallowing one last time before releasing the flesh to fall with a wet thud onto the hairy stomach.

John kneeled between the man's legs and hoisted a beefy leg over his left shoulder, noting the giant foot was longer than his face, and nuzzled a smooth pec against the man's hamstrings. He planted his right foot on the floor, spreading the man's legs farther apart until the stranger's other leg wrapped naturally as a river's bend around John's slender hip.

The room was silent and dark but for the few lights left on for security's sake. Nobody could see this far back into the restaurant and John felt safe with the man in the emptiness. He leaned forward, the stranger's ass rising with his stretched leg, and John positioned himself. He roved the furry cleft until he felt the kiss of the man's burning hole, and entered without resistance, piercing to the hilt with a victorious grunt matched by the stranger below him.

They sighed.

John caressed the shin over his shoulder, going with and then against the direction of the hair, and felt the man flex his foot as he adjusted to the length inside of him. John pushed down on the man's lower leg, opening him wider; he blinked at where they joined, his cock a bridge between them.

The man clasped John's straining thigh with a huge hand and nodded.

John let fall a viscous drop of spit onto his shaft and sheathed his dick into the man's ass centimeter by centimeter, the slipperiness stealing his breath. "You...feel...amazing..." He arched his back and then gazed down at the man, admiring the sharp, masculine planes of his face and the gray granite beard. John rolled his pelvis, easy as a ship on calm seas, while holding his upper torso still.

The man swallowed and licked his lips. "You feel good."

John increased his speed as the man relaxed, his pre-cum sleeking the stranger's insides enough for him to jackhammer into this monolith who submitted to him, who jolted with each raw thrust. There was nothing quite as intoxicating to John as seeing a strong man open himself to him.

The stranger reached behind his head and braced himself against the wall, exposing the wet curls of hair in his sweaty pits. John clutched the slab of chest with one hand, kneading it. He inhaled the clean and male scent bathing him and it whipped him faster, driving him deeper into inchoate madness where nothing existed except the fucking.

The stranger's cock, jutting from the brambles of grizzled pubic hair, slapped drunkenly on his stomach and leaked pre-cum, matting his silvered treasure trail.

John spat on his hand and grasped him. The man's pale eye widened as his staff engorged with blood, swelling to bursting as John stroked him.

"That's it...that's it...that's it..." The man threw his arm over his face, the gold band glinting faintly in the dim light. "That's it..."

John tightened his fist and jerked faster. He slammed with abandon into the moaning stranger and then leaned forward, folding the poor man in half and jamming two greasy, salty fingers into his mouth. John's eyes rolled back at the sensation of the man's circling tongue and primal sucking. He yanked his fingers away and growled in the man's face. "I'm going to fill you at both ends." John locked his lips on the stranger, invading his mouth with an unforgiving tongue that fucked the man's mouth with the ferocity his cock fucked his ass. John pounded harder, feeling the puffs of breath shoved out of the stranger with each thrust. He lengthened his strokes, every muscle in him on fire and unquenchable by the sweat streaming from his pores, and would not relent in his quest to get as deep as he could into the man where he could leave a part of himself until the stranger underneath him howled and bolts of liquid lightning covered their abdomens.

The stranger's ass clenched as the air grew pungent with the smell of his spunk and this removed the last of John's control. He roared and shot inside the man, over and over, each agonizing spasm torturous and unstoppable, emptying and filling a void in his heart.

John collapsed and they lay there, gulping air together with the desperation of caught fish with no thrash in them left.

After a while, John propped himself up and smiled at the stranger. "You need a job?"

The man chuckled and John's dick twitched. "I got one now, but thanks."

"Of course." John nodded, more to reassure himself that it was okay he had asked. "I'm going to get us some paper napkins to wipe up."

"I'm happy marinating. No rush."

John grinned and padded into the kitchen on his way to the storeroom where the to-go supplies were kept. He picked up their bowls, beer bottles, and chopsticks and placed everything in their proper receptacles—the sink, the recycling, and the trash. His body tingled. He smiled to himself and glanced up at the image of the jolly Kitchen God. "Thanks. Tomorrow, I'm getting you a pomelo."

When John returned with the napkins, the stranger had vanished. The front door was locked and he had not passed John on the way out the back door where they had first entered—he would have seen him. Without even a name to call the man, John stood there, lost as a child in a crowd.

He staggered to the booth and plunked down. Something jingled behind him, near the wall, and he turned around to find eight gold rings, identical to the armband worn by the stranger, toppled over on the seat as if they had once formed a tower. Underneath lay a note scratched in angular printing on a to-go menu:

PERHAPS A VACATION TO DENMARK?
P.S. I'LL PUT IN A GOOD WORD FOR YOU.

The Brownie Will Help

Steve Cave

"Did you like it, Jake?" Paul's mouth quirked to one side as he watched my face. His black eyebrows were raised, wrinkling his forehead. He looked concerned, which was cute, considering he was older than me. I can't even get a full beard—just patchy blonde shit that I end up shaving off.

"Yeah," I said, smiling back. "It was delicious. You made that?" I knew that he did, and it was good and all, but not *that* good. But I was glad that he'd invited me over. I'd been at his place for a couple of hours, but nothing had happened yet. He'd been nice, and a gentleman. I guess that's nice, but it's not really what I was hoping for, to be honest.

I reached over the table and brushed my fingertips along the back of his hand. His skin was rough and soft at the same time, the way a man's hands ought to feel. He turned his hand over and brushed his fingertips against my palm. The rush of feeling flooded up my arm and my breath caught. I shivered, looked him in the eye, and bust out laughing.

"Looks like the brownie's finally kicking in," he said, grinning back.

An hour before when I had first walked into his apartment, he had given me a tour of his little place that he shared with a roommate, a girl named Jessica who wasn't home. He offered me a pot brownie that he'd made. I hesitated. I'd been having a shitty time lately at my job—I work at Costco, chasing down empty carts in the parking lot all day—and had been getting stoned pretty much every day after work. I had even been skipping seeing friends, just cuz I was stoned and watching junk on Netflix that I couldn't care less about, so the previous week I had decided to give smoking a break.

But this wasn't exactly smoking. Plus, he said he'd made it, and I didn't want to be rude, right? And god damn but those thick eyebrows were so manly. It was heavy on chocolate, which was perfect. I usually just smoke because no one can ever get edibles to not taste a little like ass. But this one was rich, really rich. I'm a sucker for a guy who makes good food, since I don't cook at all.

Shit, I realized right after eating it that if it lasts as long as edibles usually do, there was no way I could drive home. I hoped he wouldn't mind me crashing here, if I had to. I hoped he'd want me to...things didn't go quite so great when we first met.

That had been up at Turkey Point a few months back. I'd finally graduated, and was ready to get out and have some real fun. Kenji was the only other gay kid I knew, but he was a bottom too so we'd settled for just being friends. I mean, I was pretty sure I was a bottom. It's hard to tell when you're a virgin, but I fingered myself a lot when I jacked off, and that's gotta mean something, right? I loved the feel of rubbing my fingertip around the outside of my hole, and then licking my finger and pushing it into me as far as it could go. I'd finger myself like that and jack off, watching porn and imagining one of the studs on top of me, pounding my ass.

My finger never went in deep enough.

Small towns suck to grow up in. There's just no guys. Well, there's guys, plenty of sexy rednecks and stuff, but they're all way too straight. Chatting with hot guys on Scruff they'd all joke about getting those guys stoned and seeing how straight they really were, but how the hell do you do that?

So it was just Kenji and me getting stoned together. We tried to fool around but mostly just jacked off together. What else is there to do in a Podunk town? Go bowling? Gee, thanks.

Kenji told me about this gay campground a few hours away where guys walked around naked and fucked wherever they wanted. It sounded hot, like living in a porn. I imagined huge muscle bears sucking and fucking in the woods. Who wouldn't want that?

The truth was that when I got there, I was scared out of my mind. At that point, Kenji's finger was the only thing I'd had in my ass besides my own fingers. Thinking back, I should have ordered a dildo off Amazon, but even that freaked me out. The one time I convinced Kenji to try, he jammed his finger in my ass way too fast, and it hurt like a motherfucker. Game over. That seems to be my thing. I'll get to that in a minute.

The guys at Turkey Point weren't exactly like I'd imagined, either. A few were hot, some were definitely not. But the way they looked at me, I felt hot. I felt like bearbait. It was a good feeling, just kind of overwhelming. Luckily there were drinks everywhere. I'm guessing that they were free...thinking back, no one stopped me, so hopefully that was the case. The first PBR helped me relax, the second, and I took off my hoodie. The third, and I was down to my Enjoi t-shirt with the pandas fucking, Timberland boots and white jockstrap. It was a real jock, Bike brand, from when I played baseball for all of a year. I sucked at it, but goddamn that locker room smelled good.

I went off to piss by the treeline, and clomped my way, looking for Kenji because he had the pot. I'm not a big guy, so I'm guessing that's why the beer hit me so hard? I'm not really sure. Drinking isn't usually my thing. With pot, there's no hangover, no problems. It's just better. Anyway, I'm clomping my way back to look for Kenji when he finds me first, and tells me about a guy who was checking out my ass while I pissed. He pointed the guy out—big, maybe a few years older, thick black scruffy face and shaggy black hair. He was wearing a jock too. He had the build of a guy who probably used to play football. *Used* to. He was definitely hot, and grinning at me while Kenji pointed at him with all the subtlety of a pimp.

I think I waved? Something stupid like that, and shoved Kenji off and plodded back to hang out at a campfire, totally embarrassed. Kenji followed me and luckily he still had his pipe with him, so we smoked a bowl. It really took the edge off of the weirdness of the place.

Later that night, I saw that guy again, and by then I was drunk and stoned enough to not give a shit. So I talked to him. His name was Paul. I don't know who kissed who first, but once it started we were licking and tasting each other like animals. His arms, his chest, all of him felt so thick and heavy. He led me back to his tent where we fell onto his air mattress with more kissing and licking and I think he was even growling at one point. I was into it. He smelled like beer and sweat and *man*. I pawed at his bulge, feeling his cock get thick in my hand. Fuck, THAT was hot. He wanted me. And his dick wasn't small, either.

I bent over and mouthed his cock through his jock and breathed in the sweet musky smell of his balls. I'd never smelled anything so good in my life. He reached a hand down to my ass, gripped a cheek, and slowly slid a finger into my ass crack. I moaned onto his cock, pushing my ass back against that thick finger. Being stoned heightened everything. I was lost in the stink of his crotch while he moved the tip of his finger in circles around my asshole.

Without warning he rolled me onto my belly. We weren't talking at all. We were both animals, and he was gonna take what he wanted. I tried to relax, and gripped the edges of the air mattress. I wanted it, but fuck I was nervous even through the cloud of being high. I didn't tell him I hadn't ever been fucked before. I didn't want to ruin it.

I heard him spit, and felt warm wetness strike my hole. He kept that finger rubbing around the entrance and I moaned and pushed back. God, it felt so good to have this stud touching me. I heard him spit again, and then I felt something push at my hole.

I wanted to relax. I wanted him to fuck me. I wanted it to be hot and sexy, like in the porn I jacked off to every fucking night. The fact that it was bareback, in the woods, with a stranger—yeah, in hind sight that probably wasn't the smartest, but fuck I wanted him.

But the pain. Holy hell it hurt so badly. I had no idea. Aching agony exploded through my body, shooting up from my ass. It was like I'd been stabbed, or shot, or...I have no idea. Without even thinking, I jerked away and cried out. I heard a ripping sound, then a whistle and whoosh and the air mattress was suddenly flat on the rocky ground beneath us.

I fucking popped his air mattress.

He laughed it off but I was horrified. I told him I didn't feel good, kept saying how sorry I was, and scrambled out of his tent. Back in my own tent, I climbed into my sleeping bag alone, and pathetic. Kenji never came back to the tent. I was sure he was out there getting fucked, having a great time. Goddamnit. I tried to jack off but couldn't, and fell asleep pissed.

He had found me the next morning. I was hung over and eating a sloppy bowl of fruit loops. I'm sure that I looked like shit. Like I said, I hardly ever drank. He settled into the chair next to mine, and said, "You sleep okay? Feeling better?"

I gave him one raised eyebrow. "I feel like shit."

"You look adorable."

I looked like a mud flap. "Thanks," I managed. "How about you? You had to sleep on the ground, huh?"

He laughed, picked up a stick and poked the fire. "I would have slept better with you."

That felt good to hear, but it was hard to believe. "I'm sorry," I said lamely.

He turned his whole face and looked directly at me and said, "Me too."

God he was a charmer. And something about that scruff, those eyebrows, that smile that split his whole face. I ended up giving him my number before Kenji and I headed out, but didn't expect to ever hear from him.

"I'm surprised that you wanted to hang out," I said to him across his dining room table, our hands still lightly touching. "I mean, after I bolted."

"Of course I called you," he said.

I wanted to say something, in case he was worried about trying again, but I had no idea what to say, so of course I said, "I'll do better this time," and immediately wanted to slug myself. What the hell?!

His lopsided grin split his face again, and he said, "The brownie will help." He reached his hand up and gently ran his thumb along the fuzz of my cheek. The touch felt good. Really good. "Come on," he said.

We stood up and picked up our dishes. As I stood, I could feel that nice stoned tingle in my legs. They felt heavy, like they were made of metal, but buzzed like they were covered in bees. Not bad bees—friendly ones.

This is the kind of shit that wanders through my head when I'm stoned.

Putting my dishes in the sink in the kitchen, I started notic-
ing that geometric pattern on stuff around me. Surfaces slid and
moved, but didn't. That brownie was strong.

I was staring at the countertop, maybe for just a moment,
maybe longer, when I noticed my cock. I was rock hard. That's not
usual for me when stoned, but something about this time, fuck I
was ready without even realizing it. Maybe it was Paul. Can you
put Viagra in a brownie? I turned to face him, and ran my palm
down his belly to his crotch. He was hard too, and damn he was
big. I looked up into his big brown eyes and he kissed me, wrapping his arms around my shoulders and pulling me in, crushing
me and my cock against him. His mouth tasted like garlic bread
and cheese.

His big paw of a hand found my cock too, and I was lost in the
feeling. Just him holding my dick, I was in heaven. He slipped his
hand into my pants, under my dick and held my balls. God it felt
like nothing I'd ever felt before. I moaned into his mouth, and
laughed.

He pulled back, smiled at me and said, "Horny, huh?"

All I could do was moan back. I was grinding into his hand at
this point. That's when the stud opened my belt with his other
hand, opened my pants and pulled out my cock. He dropped to
one knee and swallowed my dick, wrapping his hot mouth around
it while still playing with my balls with his other hand. He used
his mouth to stroke my cock, and I know I moaned loudly then.
I braced myself, holding onto his head and shoulders while he
pumped by dick up and down. I could feel his tongue roll around
the head, then underneath the shaft even licking my balls as he
took my whole dick down his throat, choking slightly.

He pulled up off of my dick and looked up into my eyes. "You
like that?"

"Fuck." I wanted to say more, but that's all that managed to
make it out of my mouth.

He laughed, licked his finger, and swallowed my dick again, but this time he slid a hand around and played with my hole with his wet finger. My legs started to shake and buckle, and he pulled off my dick again, grinned at me and stood up.

His eyes were lazy stoned, his smile lopsided. "Come on," he mumbled, and turned to walk to his room. He held my dick on one hand like a leash and I followed him like a puppy.

Next to his huge king-sized bed, we both stripped down as fast as we could. I got naked fastest, and climbed up onto the bed and lay on my back playing with my balls while I watched him finish stripping. His dick was straining against his red briefs, up and to the side, looking thick. He grabbed the hem of his t-shirt and pulled it up and over his head slowly, revealing his furry pecs and belly. I was jacking now with one hand, feeling my balls with the other, and slipping a finger down to touch my hole, watching this stud smile and rip his clothed off for me. He hooked his thumbs into his waistband and yanked the underwear down, letting his dick flop out. He flexed his arms as he did this, and fuck he looked like a porn star.

His cock was cut, and I have no idea, but maybe eight inches? Maybe more? It looked massive. He did a little hop on one foot to get the red underwear all the way off. It was cute. I giggled, and so did he.

Then, while nude, his smile became something predatory.

He put a knee up on the bed, and then walked over to me on his knees, body upright, grabbing his dick in one fist and stroking it slowly. He moved on his knees up beside my head and looked down, pushing his cock towards my face. The smile was completely gone, burned up in lust.

I scooted over, still stroking my dick with one hand, and gently took ahold of his dick with my other. He let out a gasp at my touch. It was so incredibly sexy, this big stud of a man, wanting me, being turned on by me.

I licked the tip of his dick, and me moaned louder. I looked up at him again, but his head was back. I opened my mouth and wrapped my lips around the swollen head of his cock. He tasted clean this time, but there was still a smell here, his sweet masculine musk. I loved it.

I slid my mouth down on his dick, rubbing my tongue along the bottom like he had done for me, squishing my mouth around it, licking and sucking. I moved my head forwards and back, pumping his dick with my mouth. It all just seemed natural.

Being stoned, I was fully in that moment, enjoying feeling his cock in my mouth, enjoying the taste and smell of him. The fact that this was the first cock I'd ever sucked didn't hit me until later. Right then nothing mattered except what was happening. And right then, he was all that was. His dick was so big, I could hold it with one hand while going down on it as far as I could.

Well, as far as I thought I could. I felt those big hands of his on the back on my head, and he pushed me down on his cock even further. I gagged, and he pulled back, but then pushed me back down again. I got a little further that time, but only a little. I'd never had anything that big in my throat before. He humped my face like this for a while. It hurt but somehow it was also sexy as fuck. I'm sure being stoned helped. I gave in to him, gagging, focusing on trying to get that thick dick down my throat as far as I could.

He pulled me off, looked down at me and asked. "You okay Jake?"

I wiped my chin. "Yeah." I had drooled a lot.

I tried to go back to sucking him, but instead Paul flopped down onto his back next to me. "C'mere," he said, half-lidded stoner eyes twinkling over that bushy scruff beard. He pulled me on top of him, so we were lying face to face, our cocks smushed between us, and kissed me. It was a deep penetrating kiss, and while he did it, I felt his thick finger reach back and rub my hole.

I moaned back into his mouth and pushed my ass against his fingers.

He pulled his mouth away from his and got some spit on those fingers, then reached back and rubbed on my hole some more. God, I could have come right there, feeling his big dick rub against mine, his fingers on my hole, his mouth on mine. He rubbed me and kissed me, both hands now on my ass, while my hands wrapped around his shaggy head.

I pulled my head back and looked down at him. His thick eyebrows raised, those damn sexy eyebrows, and I said, "I wannit."

He looked concerned. "Ya sure?"

To reply, I pushed against those fingers of his. He rolled me off of himself, and then reached over to a side table for a bottle of Fuckwater lube that he had waiting there. He rolled back to lie next to me, snapped the bottle open and poured out a healthy glob onto his dick. Then he looked back at me, put the tube aside, and said with a grin and a growl, "Then, get tha lube all over m' cock."

"Oh. Kay." I wrapped my hand around the gel, rubbing it around his fuck stick, jacking him with it.

He laid his head back and moaned for a bit, enjoying the hand job. I loved feeling his cock, so hard and yet soft in my hand.

After a bit he opened his eyes and said, "Rub the lube on yer hole."

"Oh," I said again. Everything was happening so slowly for me, but everything felt so damn good. Lubing up my ass felt amazing. I'd never used lube on my ass when I jacked off before. I don't know how I'd never thought of that.

"Hey," he said, and I opened my eyes. I'd been lost in the feeling. "Climb on." He held his thick cock upright with a thumb and finger. His face was plastered with a lustful stoned grin.

I climbed onto him and straddled his chest, and then reached back and found his dick. I stroked him a few times while watching his face. His eyes rolled back and he moaned, his hips buck-ing gently against my fist. God it was hot getting a stud like this worked up.

I stopped jacking him and leaned forward, setting the head of his dick right at my hole. I stopped, feeling that swollen mush-room head push against my asshole, and tensed up.

"Hey," he said, and I opened my eyes and looked down at him. "Relax," he said.

He put his big hands on my hips, and that touch felt so good. All of this felt so good, even his cock against my hole felt good. I pushed my hips against his cock, just a little, and felt his head slowly open up my hole. It didn't hurt yet but I tensed anyway. I looked down at Paul, at his smile, his hunger, that scruff and those eyebrows, and breathed.

I was pushing slowly, feeling flashes of pain, then waiting for them to pass, when Paul wrapped a hand around my dick. He'd lubed up his hand, so his thick fingers slid over my cock easily. He slowly jacked me, fingers squeezing a bit right at the head, and it felt like nothing I've ever felt before. I bucked against his hand and against his cock in a steady rhythm until my balls touched his furry belly. I looked down, I'm sure my eyes were wide. It hurt some, but he was in me, all the way in me, and it felt fucking awesome.

He pushed up into me and I gasped. He pushed up again, keep-ing the rhythm with his fist on my dick. Pain and pleasure mixed, while time slipped around us. I don't know how long he fucked me like that, bucking up into me while I ground down into him, picking up speed, each of us loud in our pleasure. He was hitting something deep inside me that I never knew was there. I wanted to come right away, but the feeling was too much, too overwhelm-ing. I was lost in the feeling of him fucking me for what felt like years, riding him, him thrusting up into me, his hands on my cock and ass, my hands on the tangled fur of his chest.

At one point, I raised myself up and off of him a bit, so that he could fuck me even harder, pounding my hole. He stopped jacking me and grabbed my hips. I kissed him, but the force of his cock slamming into me shoved my face forward onto his shoulder while he fucked the shit out of me. Again, time slipped and I have no idea how long he fucked me hard like that. He was sweaty. I could taste it on him. He moaned even louder at my licking and kissing under his ear and up the side of his neck. Suddenly, he gripped my ass cheeks hard, grunted loudly and thrust even harder, and I knew he was about to come.

He fucked his cock deep into me and I felt him spasm over and over inside my ass. He was coming in me, this stud, this man. It was amazing, and even the coming felt like it lasted forever.

He stopped moving, and I slid back, taking his dick all the way back inside me before he went soft. I looked down at him. He looked sweaty and spent. I ground against his cock, still hard, and a little jerking spasm ran through him. It was hot. I moved my ass up and down on his dick, fucking myself. Paul wrapped his hand back around my dick, and it didn't take long. I'd been so close the whole night, knowing that Paul's load was in buried inside me pushed me over the edge. I ground my hips down into his dick hard, again and again, moaning. I tried to tell him that I was going to come, but I think I just cried out sounds, head back, loudly, at the ceiling. He knew. He fucked me and jacked me harder.

When I came, it was from somewhere deep in my core. It was like my whole body came. I shivered, jerked, cried out and shot once, twice, and then a third time. I looked down, body still shaking and jerking, and saw the line of my cum ropes streaked up his fuzzy chest. One ran up the side of his face, just missing his eye.

He was smiling at me and said, "Good boy!"

Those words struck home. I felt spent. I felt amazing. I'd done it.

His cock was softening and I slid to the side, feeling his dick pull from my hole. I settled down to lie next to him, one leg still on top of him. He reached over and wrapped an arm around me, pulled me close to him so that my head rested on his chest. I could see the trail of my cum in his chest hair. I wrapped my free arm around him and held him, while he held me. We were sweaty, cummy and spent.

We both slept then. I don't know for how long. I woke up and inhaled, smelling cum and ass and lube and sweat, and sighed heavily. I was a little less stoned, but way more sleepy.

"You okay?" Paul's voice came from above my head, with added base from my having one ear to his chest.

"We smell like…"

"Like fucking?" I could hear the smile in his voice.

I hadn't known what fucking smelled like before this. I wanted to tell him, let him know that he was my first time, and that he was amazing, but sleep was tugging at me.

"Can I stay the night?" I managed.

In answer, Paul pulled a blanket over us from somewhere off to the side. I snuggled in tighter, breathing everything in, and fell asleep.

Skater Boys

Anonymous

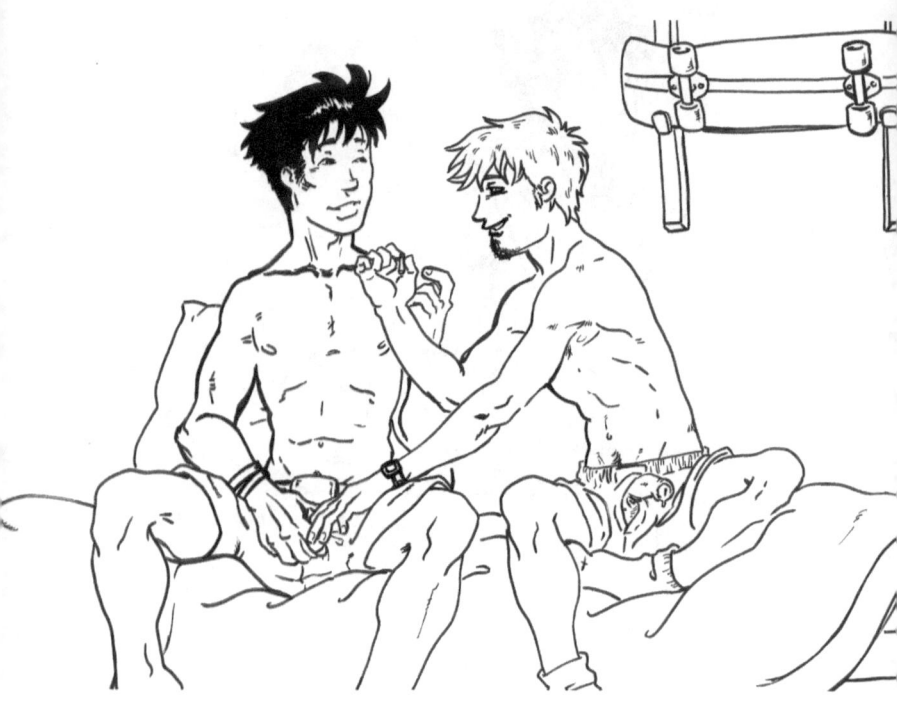

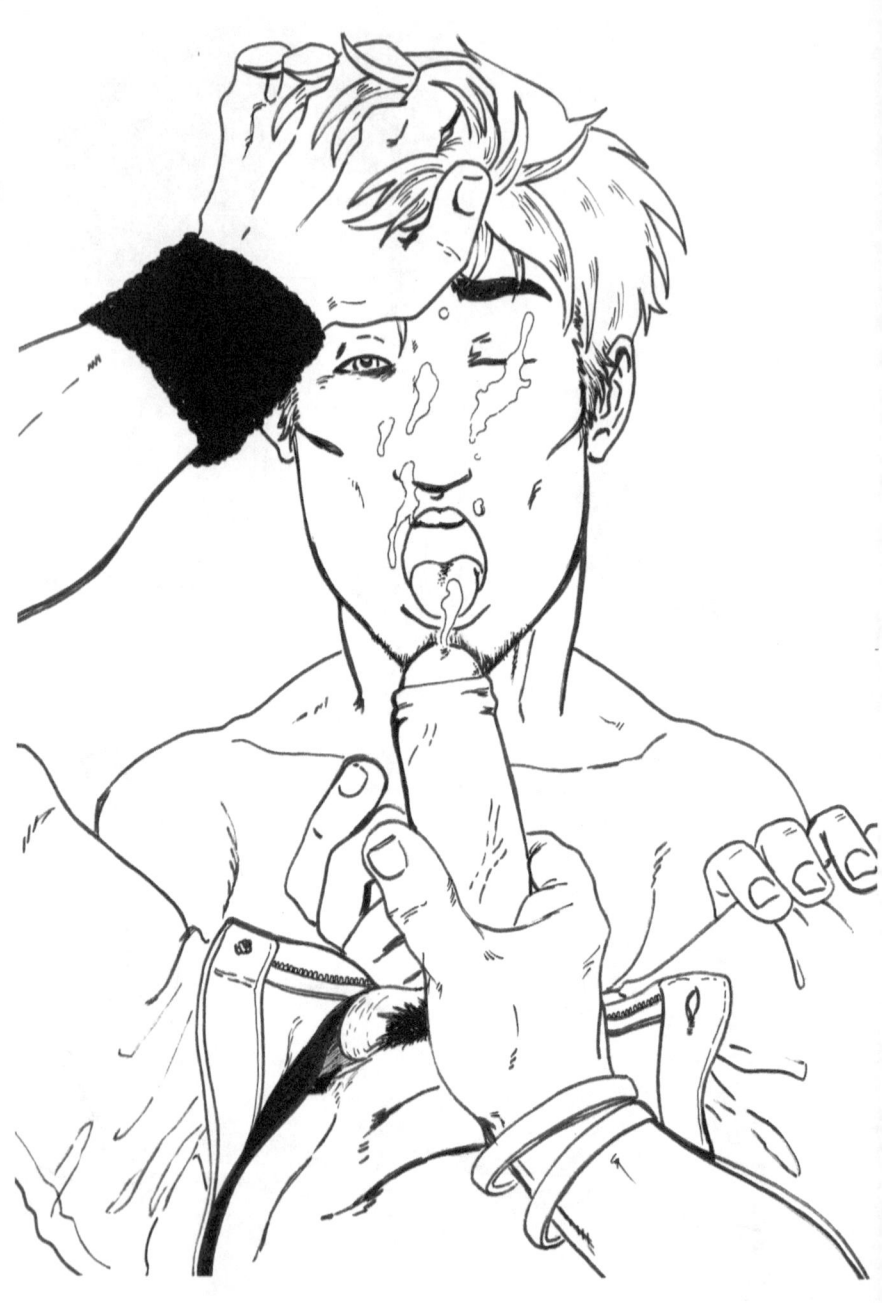

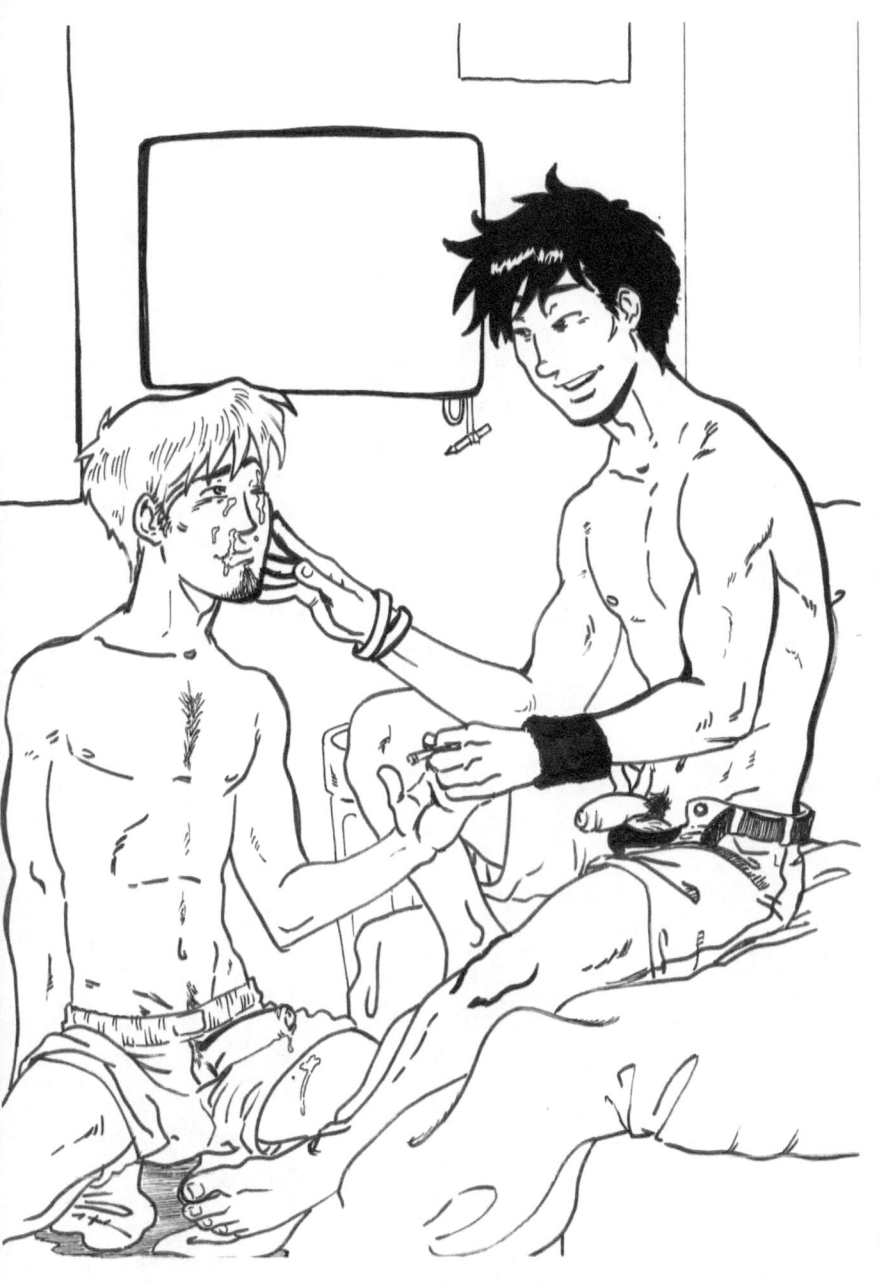

Echolocation: Summer, 2016

Niels Vonberg

*B*efore they put clothes on, Hank and Duke stared at each other—their bodies stood erect, their dicks peacefully shrunken and content. Their bodies are similar, but Duke's armpit hair are bushier and, more often than not, smellier. He never cares to use deodorant—this is rebellion against a society of external beauty, appearances and the fear of whatever is natural. It all has to be connected. Whatever is, is. Or so he says. Duke reads Rousseau at home. His room has a *Forbidden Entry* sign, which everybody respects. Duke's skin is white although his neck, arms and face are red. "Original redneck," he often jokes, after which follows a half-baked threat of what he would do if Trump were elected. They both know this kind of talking politics is the only language they have. They are still boys—young men when elderly people want to boost their self-esteem.

But if boys will be boys, their bodies are lying. The taste of Duke's sweat, semen, saliva—salty like a fishing harbour and faintly spicy—still lingers in Hank's mouth. They both had taken a drag from the joint that Duke rolled when they were still lying on Duke's bed. It seemed fitting to do this while nude because real men have no shame, Duke said earlier on. And then he laughed, which made it all into a joke. I would never grow a beard, Hank replied and Duke nodded approvingly while he inhaled deeply. Hank watched the shape of the pillows. The sheets on the bed resembled the ocean floor or large, blue plains.

Duke's eyes are focused on Hank and he squints as if he is looking for something, something carved in Hank's chest. When Hank looks at Duke's chest Hank can only distinguish four or five short hairs that could be perceived as some ancient carvings. What could they mean? The future looks dark—although Duke says that it is almost sure Clinton will win. But still. How much longer can they do this, lying bare-assed on a bed, smoking, having sex? The freedom of the body, the freedom of the mind.

"I am so in my head," Hank says.

"We should get out of here." Duke grabs some clothes from the floor and throws Hank a t-shirt. "I think this is yours."

Hank doesn't even bother to ask if they should have a shower. The shirt he got is the one with concentric circles. Hank looks at the back of the shirt, but all there is printed are circles.

"My brother got it at a concert. But the name of the band faded. Here." Duke points at some grey-white points in the middle of the front of the shirt. "Here, you see the name."

Duke's hair smells of hashish. Hank can feel his dick responding again.

"Man, you should really wash your hair," Hank says.

Duke strokes a hand carelessly through his hair. "Let's go to the beach then."

Hank pulls the shirt over his head. He looks younger, but less innocent with clothes on. Duke wears an old Metallica shirt. A monster carries a woman through a portal. The woman is asleep or dead. Drops of blood fall off her feet. The monster is either offering her or saving her.

"I'd rather have that shirt," Hank says. Duke looks at him for a moment and then takes off his shirt and swaps it for the concentric circles.

"Yeah, it does look good on me," Duke says without the conceit that one expects when somebody says something like that. He only gives himself one quick glace in the mirror before bending over to get his underwear from the floor.

They walk out of Duke's house together, which is in the middle of the village, right on the brink of the wealthy neighbourhoods and the ones where the poorer people live. Even though both Hank and Duke grew up here, they have to think about where to go. The small town they live in is a veritable suburban labyrinth. Safe for children to play anywhere, safe for families. One step in the wrong way means that you have to walk all around in order to get where you wanted or start all over again. The village is designed like that. From a bird's point of view the streets form a spiral-like map together. The only way to get out, Hank knows, is to get out of it completely.

*H*ank and Duke are walking out of their neighbourhood in what seems like the endlessly widening circles on Duke's t-shirt, although the actual walk only takes one hour usually, perhaps less. But it feels longer. It feels like they are on some kind of pilgrimage, as if they are going to a place that is not only a promise, but it will somehow set them free. It will be the beginning and the end, an answer to start a whole new way of—

Hank tries to stop thinking, and although this train of thoughts and conclusions will never stop, it fades away to the back of his mind like a low humming. Just like the insects that can now be heard, all around busying themselves, perfecting their own society. Hank's erection has disappeared, he notices. But his entire body feels bigger. He became a man this morning.

"Are you okay, buddy?" Duke voice sounds lower than usual. Maybe he's whispering.

Hank realizes that Duke's worried he might be depressed. The way Duke's looking at him. They say depression or even psychosis seen in the eyes—despite the fact that Hank does not know who "they" are. He is sure, however, that it includes the guys from school who are always after him, who stand in front of him in the locker room before or after gym and, while only wearing their boxers shorts, grabs their dicks and say: "I know you want to suck this, faggot." And of course, Hank wouldn't mind, except they are complete assholes.

He snorts his nose.

"Are you okay, buddy?" Duke lays a hand on Hank's shoulders. With the other hand, Duke wipes errant hair from his face. The sun has bleached Duke's hair this summer. It is almost white. The sideburns Duke sports reveal another colour, something in the way of red. It is not at all like his pubic hair. This keeps on surprising Hank.

"Yeah, I am okay. I should have eaten more, I think."

But despite all his thinking, they are getting out of the village. They keep on walking. They reach the outer skirts of their village where only villa's can be found. Each house has its own architectural design; there are no two copies of anything. They walk past Rinda's house.

"Rinda's parents still live there?"

"Rinda..." Duke says absentmindedly.

The sun goes down very slowly tonight.

"Yes, Rinda. We were in the same class together. We dated for a while." Hank looks away from both house and Duke as he talks.

Hank faintly recognizes a woman they pass by. Her hair is all curls, but not the natural kind. She smells of heavy, sweet perfume and has been dressed as if she's going to play tennis. She observes Hank and Duke for a moment with a twitch of suspicion, but looks away as soon as Hank stares back. He remembers. She is married to a naval officer and Hank beat up her son once for being—for being annoying, he guesses. Both her children have thick, curly hair, so perhaps he is wrong about hers.

"You mean, you dated a girl?" Duke says. "Wow, I never thought that about you."

"What do you mean, think about me?"

"Well, I mean—I didn't know you dated girls."

"I don't. I was twelve. We barely kissed."

"Oh."

They pass the street and follow another block of houses. These are bungalows that were built in the 1970s for tourists.. Most are occupied now. Clothes and towels are hanging on plastic lines. Somewhere a child screams. A father is heard and the screaming stops and is soon replaced by silence.

"I never kissed a girl before." Duke spits on the ground.

"Never?" It doesn't take Hank completely by surprise. Sure, Duke is very sexy. When Duke is at his place and lies on his bed with his arms folded, Hank cannot stop looking at his armpit hair that always shows from under the short sleeves of his t-shirt. And more so, there is always the trail of hairs on his belly that either point at Duke's chest cavity or the other way down. He fantasized about it so long…all projection, but he has never been able to see Duke as the kind of guy who will end up having a girlfriend. It also worries him slightly. Duke doesn't not look like anybody's boyfriend.

"No never. Just never met anybody. I mean, no girl. Want to go for an ice cream?" Duke points at an ice cream vendor that has been stalled at the end of the street. There are no more houses in sight. This is the end of the village. Beyond the ice cream van is only meadow, trees and a few kilometres in the distance, the dunes rise up as soft, gentle chests of sleeping bodies. Duke orders without asking what Hank wants and when Hank is getting his wallet Dukes waves him away. "My treat, man. We need something to eat."

The guy in the van bends forward over the boxes filled with ice cream in primary colours. It's the additives that do it, Hank knows. It's all something extra that fades away in the end, making things sticky and gross. Duke hands him the cone with ice scream while already licking his own.

"Are you guys going to the beach?" the ice-cream man asks. He looks at Duke first, then looks at Hank. The man resembles David Duchovny but a Duchovny with more rings around his eyes as if he has been up all night. Calluses cover both his hands. "I always went to the beach in the summer. I would just get my surfboard and that was it. You don't need much. Just your board, some beer maybe afterwards, a girl." He smiles meaningfully, but his face mutes when neither Duke nor Hank responds in kind. The ice cream melts quickly. "Here," the man says and hands over some serviettes.

"You guys already decided what to vote?"

Hank and Duke do not know what to reply. Hank shrugs his shoulders.

"You guys are allowed to vote? Did you register?"

Duke nods his head.

"They are all stuck on their own island. They only listen to each other. It's all echolocation."

"Echolocation?" Hank asks.

"Echolocation," the man repeats. "It's like the t-shirt your friend is wearing. It's all the same thing that only confirms what you already know, but there is no truth to it. They may all point to the same thing, but the point is missing, the circles only exist by means of the absence. I am telling you, it's what they want you to—"

But now Duke turns away after he has given Hank a short nod. A short flick with his head as if they are already too late for something. It is going to be a long sundown, however. The dunes are set in orange. They will need to find a bright spot.

Hank follows Duke, while the ice cream man looks at them, softly shaking his head. "Those goddamn—" But he doesn"t finish his sentence. He just stares at them, remembering a certain summer. He voted Dukakis back then. It had been a summer of masturbating. He turns away and starts locking up shop.

The road to the dunes is one straight line. Behind them the village grows smaller and smaller. The trees that surround the village become bushy sticks. They both walk backwards so they have an overview of their village. "It is just a suburb," Duke says. "One day we will get out of here."

Hank laughs, but not out loud. He enjoys the idea of "we," but cringes at the same time because of the impossibility. Nobody's boyfriend. It is as if he's holding back a door. "Where would you like to go to?"

"I don't know. We could go to the city and get a place together if you want to."

"Live together? I mean—"

Duke interrupts Hank. "My brother lives together with a friend. They each have separate bedrooms and share a living room. It's much cheaper that way. We could do that." They turn around with their face towards the orange dunes.

And so Hank is right. Everything they do together is just a game or something. "I never thought about it." Yet, it's not difficult to imagine them living together in one house. They could watch movies together all night long and smoke their brains out while lying next to each other on the couch like they sometimes do when Duke's or Hank's parents are gone. It could be exactly like what it was now.

Duke's face is pink with orange from the sun. The one mole on his cheek almost disappears in those colours. "I mean, we could watch movies all night and smoke some."

Who would be the first one to reach for the other's zipper? Hank wonders.

Duke chuckles. It echoes strangely against the pavement.

A car drives past with a family of four. Tourists obviously. For a moment Hank and Duke watch the children who seem to be sleeping in the backseat. The father behind the wheel with his hand through the open window on the car door outside as if he is holding a delicate balance with the children sleeping and his wife staring out of the front window looking angry. The summer sun is able to unleash so many unbalances of family life.

"Are you parents still having arguments?" Hank asks.

Duke shakes his head, but doesn't say anything. He kicks a stone. It shoots forward in a curve. A passing car rides over it. "They just do their thing. But it's calm now. My brother often calls me."

They pass the street and walk up the dunes. The road to the beach is empty, but then, this is not a favourite spot for tourists. A couple of miles further away, there is another entrance to the beach with a bar-dancing and restaurants.

Hank follows Duke, who starts to climb a dune. Within minutes they are surrounded by sand and beachgrass. "There! There!" Duke says and points to a spot in the distance. The run off a dune and climb a new one. Their feet are sucked by sand and they need to use strength to pull them out. When Duke runs off a new dune top, he lets himself fall into the sandpit and lies still on his back. Hank carefully walks off the dune and makes sure that sand is not falling in Duke's face. He lies down next to Duke.

His nose is inches from Duke's armpit. While a sweet smell of hashish rises from the fabric of Duke's shirt, it's the soft, salty smell of those coarse hairs that appeals to Hank the most.

Duke starts to play with Hank's hair. "Has your hair always been this thick? It's so thick man."

Hank listens to the waves. Seagulls are pouring their shouts over them. He starts to get a boner again. Duke's jeans are too big. There is a gap between his waist and his jeans and Hank sees Duke is wearing his red shorts.

Duke begins stroking Hank's neck. With his eyes closed, Hank feels Duke's fingers running across his neck, each muscle loosening, touching, his fingers being huge, soft spades that run through his skin as though everything has become palpable, liquid almost. Hank can feel the touches grow and reach his spine.

A couple of seagulls are nearby.

Duke removes his arms and gets up. "Want some, buddy?" From the pocket of his jeans he pulls out a plastic tube in which he has saved a joint.

Hank sits up. Duke unrolls the lid and shakes the plastic tube in his hand until the joint falls out of it. "Be careful," Hank says, "we don't want any sand on it."

Duke lights up his zipper and burns the tip of the joint and takes a deep breath. He holds his breath for a while and then lets out a long stream of smoke. He immediately offers Hank the joint, who repeats Duke's movement. The pass the joint to and throw as if they are spooning from the same bowl of soup. This must be an old routine, Hank thinks, there must be some kind of continuity. Yet, they are all alone here. There is nobody else in the dunes here who can interrupt their moment of peace nor can they be part of it. It is pure selfishness. I want him. Hank knows this and then lets the thought go. I want him. The feeling remains.

Duke sits up straight. Hank recognizes the way Duke moves, the way he sits up now. His back straight, his hair falling over his ears, his eyes two slits from which he watches Hank. As if Duke knows everything about him.

I am afraid, Hank knows, but he holds his back straight as well and doesn't move when Duke bends over and gives him a kiss. His lips press against Hank's and his tongue goes inside and without thinking about Hank replies the movement of Duke's tongue by circling his own tongue around his. Duke presses Hank backwards, but it is a gentle press. Hank is allowed to resist, but doesn't. Duke falls on him and he doesn't stop kissing, but instead wraps his arms around Hank and by means of positing his waist and crotch on Hank, he makes Hank spread his legs a bit.

When he stops kissing, Duke stares down at Hank. He's seeking something in Hank's eyes. "Let's do it again," Duke says. "I hope you feel okay with that."

Hank only nods.

"I thought so."

Duke rolls off Hank and lights up the joint again and starts smoking it. It's becoming dark. The tip of the joint lights up every time Duke inhales. The grey smoke lingers around longer than usual behind which Duke's smile floats invitingly every time he exhales.

Hank starts to undress himself.

About the Contributors

ANONYMOUS is a less-than-famous illustrator who enjoys drawing cute guys in various states of arousal.

STEVE BERMAN is the author of numerous short stories (oft-collected in *Trysts*, *Second Thoughts*, *Red Caps*, and the forthcoming *Fit for Consumption*) and the young adult novel, *Vintage: A Ghost Story*. He resides in Western Massachusetts, which allows recreational marijuana, though he's so uptight it's unsure if he will ever indulge.

STEVE CAVE is a big scruffy guy who lives in Seattle, and who recently wrangled his MFA in Creative Writing. He spends a lot of his time teaching at City University and running a small tabletop games company that he launched last year called Cavewolf Games. The rest of his time is spent mostly goofing off, making "art," and writing everything from science fiction to creative non-fiction to erotica.

TRISH DeVENE's fiction and poetry have appeared in the anthologies *The Cougar Book*; *Nice Girls, Naughty Sex*; *Flesh*

Made Word; Blurring the Line; Like a Chill Down Your Spine; and *Queer Fish 2;* as well as in numerous magazines, including *Rose and Thorn, Clean Sheets, Oysters and Chocolate,* and *Scarlet Literary Magazine.*

*J*OHN DUMAS lives in Southern California with his husband. He has a degree in English and Medieval Studies, but used to do IT support. This is his first published story.

*J*ACKSON DUPOINT hails from Tampa, Florida. Along with being unapologetically bisexual, he is in the process of writing an upcoming short story collection.

L.A. FIELDS is the author of The Disorder Series, the short story collection *Countrycide*, the Lambda Literary Award finalist *My Dear Watson, Homo Superiors*, a modern retelling of Chicago's Leopold and Loeb crime, and an annotated edition of *Joseph and His Friend*, the first American gay novel.

*A*LEX JEFFERS's pornographic fairy tale *The Padişah's Son and the Fox* won a Lambda Literary Award. He has seven other books in print. "His First Time" is excerpted from an as-yet-untitled sword & sorcery novel in progress which he is serializing at www.patreon.com/Alex_Jeffers

*P*HILLIP JOY lives in Nova Scotia in a house of bears and books. He is currently working on his PhD in gay men's health. In his time away from writing his dissertation, he enjoys writing gay erotica. This is his second short story to be published; you can read his first in *His Seed: An Arboretum of Gay Erotica.*

*C*HARLES PAYSEUR is an avid reader, writer, and reviewer of all things speculative. His fiction and poetry have appeared at *Strange Horizons*, *Lightspeed Magazine*, *The Book Smugglers*, and many more. He runs Quick Sip Reviews and can be found drunkenly reviewing Goosebumps on his Patreon. You can find him gushing about short fiction (and occasionally his cats) on Twitter as @ClowderofTwo.

*N*ELSON STANLEY works in an academic library in rural Cornwall, UK. His stories have been published recently in places like *Black Dandy*, *Tough Crime Magazine*, *The Gallery of Curiosities* and *The Sockdolager*. One of his stories was included in the British Fantasy Award-winning anthology *Extended Play*.

*N*IELS VONBERG graduated six years ago in Amsterdam on a researchmaster Literature. After graduating, he started to focus on writing short stories—in English and Dutch. Several reviews and articles were published on Dutch websites such as *Tijdschrift LOVER* and *Literair Nederland*. In 2017 he moved to the Swedish coast and has started to work at the local art museum for which he also writes blogs.

T.P. WATCHER has written some very evocative stories and been kind enough to share them with the world through Nifty.org.

*A*TOM YANG was born to Chinese immigrant parents who thought it'd be a hoot to raise him as an immigrant, too—so he grew up estranged in a familiar land, which gives him an interesting perspective. He's named after a Japanese manga (comic book) character, in case you were wondering.

About the Editor

A native of Boulder, BUD KUSH shows up unannounced a good deal. He always shares with friends, he always put in money for snacks; he hums after taking a hit from a bong. Black mote—marijuana blended with honey—is his preferred vice. Oh, and men. Lots and lots of men. They're not bad with honey, too.

www.ingramcontent.com/pod-product-compliance
Lightning Source LLC
Chambersburg PA
CBHW031408250626
47155CB00004B/1462